# BUDDY IS A STUPID NAME FOR A GIRL

BOOKS BY WILLO DAVIS ROBERTS

*The View from the Cherry Tree*

*Don't Hurt Laurie!*

*The Minden Curse*

*More Minden Curses*

*The Girl with the Silver Eyes*

*The Pet-sitting Peril*

*Baby-sitting Is a Dangerous Job*

*No Monsters in the Closet*

*Eddie and the Fair Godpuppy*

*The Magic Book*

*Sugar Isn't Everything*

*Megan's Island*

*What Could Go Wrong?*

*Nightmare*

*To Grandmother's House We Go*

*Scared Stiff*

*Jo and the Bandit*

*What Are We Going to Do about David?*

*Caught!*

*The Absolutely True Story . . . How I Visited Yellowstone Park with the Terrible Rupes*

*Twisted Summer*

*Secrets at Hidden Valley*

*The Kidnappers*

*Pawns*

*Hostage*

*Buddy Is a Stupid Name for a Girl*

# BUDDY IS A STUPID NAME FOR A GIRL

## Willo Davis Roberts

A JEAN KARL BOOK

ATHENEUM BOOKS FOR YOUNG READERS

*New York London Toronto Sydney Singapore*

Atheneum Books for Young Readers
An imprint of Simon & Schuster Children's Publishing Division
1230 Avenue of the Americas
New York, New York 10020

The text of this book is set in Granjon.

Printed in the United States of America

10  9  8  7  6  5  4  3  2  1

*Library of Congress Cataloging-in-Publication Data*
Roberts, Willo Davis.
Buddy is a stupid name for a girl / Willo Davis Roberts.
   p. cm.
"A Jean Karl book."
Summary: When her father disappears mysteriously on a trucking job,
eleven-year-old Buddy moves in with relatives she hardly knows and
finds herself in a dysfunctional family with secrets about the past.
   ISBN 0-689-81670-7
[1. Aunts—Fiction. 2. Grandfathers—Fiction. 3. Old age—Fiction.
4. Alcoholism—Fiction. 5. Mystery and detective stories.] I. Title.
PZ7.R54465 Bu 2001
[Fic]—dc21            99-087471

# BUDDY
# IS A STUPID
# NAME FOR
# A GIRL

# 1

She had always liked the landlord, Mr. Bea-man. Until today. Buddy watched his mouth as he talked, and she hated him.

"If your dad don't show up," he said, "you know, in a reasonable period of time, I can call Washington Social Services for you. They know what to do about kids who don't have anywhere to go."

Buddy didn't have to look at her brother to see that he shared her feelings about that. Being put in a foster home, or a shelter? There wasn't even a shelter, as far as she knew, except in the big cities like Tacoma or Seattle, away. And she was sure Dad wouldn't want them to resort to anything like that.

Mr. Beaman must have read their rejection in their faces. He switched tactics. "You kids got relatives. Idaho, ain't it? Or Montana, someplace like that. Go to them. That's the thing to do."

Beside her, Bart stood stiff and frozen in shock. The same shock Buddy was feeling, only her brother didn't speak.

"We can't go to Montana," Buddy exclaimed. "They don't even write to us, didn't write much even before Mama died."

Mr. Beaman licked his lips and looked miserable. "Still, they're family. You're just kids. They'll look after you. See, the thing is . . . you're two months behind on the rent now. And . . . well, you know I lost my job, too, when the mill closed. Same as your dad. I need the rent money. And . . . I got a family wants to rent the house. They got cash, first month and a deposit. I . . . told 'em they could move in Friday, first of the month."

Bart looked as if he were frozen. His lips barely moved. "I don't think . . . it's not legal to just throw us out with no notice."

"Well, you know and I know you haven't paid me any rent for almost three months. That's notice enough to be legal, I reckon. I need the money myself. I have to take this while I got the chance."

"But you told my dad—"

"He said he'd get money to me before this. I can't wait any longer," Mr. Beaman said with determination, even though he was looking somewhat guilty. "You're gonna have to move, anyway, right, if the only job he could find is out of town? So you're gonna have to get out of the house before I lose these renters."

Buddy couldn't believe what she was hearing. "But we can't go to Haysville," she told him, glancing at her brother in the hope he'd back her up. "We have to wait until Dad comes back!"

The man licked his lips again. "I'm sorry," he said. "I already told 'em. Monday, I said."

She felt as if she were drowning, suffocating. Bart made a strangling sound, and finally spoke in a voice that wasn't like his at all. "We couldn't take all our stuff with us. Not in a car."

"No, no, I realize that. You can store it in the garage. I told the new people you wouldn't be able to clear that out yet. You don't own any of the furniture, so just pack the rest of it. Get some boxes at the Stop and Shop. They always have boxes."

And then he was gone, letting the door slam behind him, down the front steps to his car. Buddy glared after him through the sting of tears. "What're we going to do?" she demanded.

Bart rubbed a hand across his mouth. "Get out, I guess."

"But Dad won't know where to find us when he comes back!"

"We only got relatives in one town. He'd call them if he couldn't find us here. But we don't have to go yet. We . . . we could manage in the car for a day or two, couldn't we? Park near the bus station. It's open all night. We could use the bathroom there, just for a couple of days. Watch for Dad, if he comes in on the bus."

"Sleep in the car? Like we're homeless?" Her voice squeaked.

Bart looked her straight in the face. "Buddy, we *are* homeless. Until Dad comes back."

She cried then. How could anybody live in a *car?* No bathroom, no kitchen, no room to stretch out to sleep? How would they cook? How would they stay clean? How could they go to school?

Bart was watching her with hurting eyes. "It wouldn't be for long," he said. "At least Dad left the car. We won't be on the street."

"Can't we consult a lawyer? I don't care what he said, it can't be legal to just put us out on the street!"

"I don't think it is, but how would we pay a lawyer? If we could afford one, we'd have paid the rent. And he's right about our having to move pretty soon, anyway. Dad said we probably wouldn't be able to stay here if he had to work out of Lewiston."

Buddy was terrified. But there didn't seem to be any choices to speak of. The next day they didn't go to school. Instead, Bart brought home a carload of boxes, and they started packing everything they'd have to move out of the rented house.

She kept on drizzling all through the job. Tears

ran down her cheeks, and she wiped them on the sleeve of her sweatshirt. Her nose ran, too. The tissues had already been packed somewhere, so she used toilet paper to wipe her nose, but eventually she opened the box she'd packed the Kleenex in and kept it out. She figured they'd better have it in the car.

A car doesn't hold much. Pillows, they decided, and a couple of blankets apiece. Food that wouldn't spoil without refrigeration and didn't need to be cooked.

Buddy looked drearily at her brother, who was putting books into a carton and sealing it. "What about clothes?" she asked.

"Keep it simple. Jeans and shirts, a jacket in case it's cold. Stuff that doesn't have to be hung up. Things you can wear more than once without washing. Socks and underwear. If we have to, we can wash those out in the rest room at the bus station."

"What about this?" she asked as she picked up Mama's photo album. "In with the books? It has the only pictures of her except for that big one Dad has on his nightstand. Maybe we ought to keep it with us."

Bart's expression didn't change. It was closed, cold, keeping in the hurt. "We don't have room for it, Buddy. We can't take anything in the car we don't absolutely have to have."

She couldn't bring herself to put it in with the books. She sank down on the floor, Indian fashion, and opened the big album flat on her legs. "Look. There's Mom when she was my age. With Aunt Cassie and Aunt Addie."

Bart didn't answer. He closed that box and pulled over another one.

Buddy leafed through the snapshots. Mama and Dad before they were married. Aunt Adelaide when she graduated from high school, with her hair in stiff curls, thin and wearing a smile. And her wedding picture, when she married Uncle Ed, who died. They all went to his funeral when Buddy was about six. Mama didn't cry, but she hugged Aunt Addie.

She flipped through the pages, stirring up memories. Some of the older pictures were of people she didn't know, or at least didn't remember. But she could pick out Aunt Cassie. She was shorter than Addie, and rounder, with a pretty, laughing face. There was one of her with Mama, their arms around each other, making silly faces at the camera.

And a formal picture, taken by a professional photographer, of Grandpa Dolan. He had died before Buddy was even born, so she didn't remember him. But she remembered Grandpa Harry. The picture of him showed an old man, tall and thin and elegant in a white suit, leaning slightly on a cane. He was really their great-grandpa, and he'd been very old when she'd seen him last. He had owned the Ostrom Appliance and Hardware Store in Haysville, and he always had butterscotch drops wrapped in cellophane in his pockets for visiting kids.

Buddy turned a page and saw snapshots of Bart and then herself as babies and later as toddlers. She'd been fat then, and so had Bart.

Suddenly the album was jerked out of her hands. "Come on, Buddy, we've got to get this done," Bart said, and jammed it into the box of books he was working on.

They packed dishes and bedding and towels. They packed Dad's clothes, and labeled all the cartons so they could find things in a hurry when Dad wanted them. He'd only taken a small bag with him.

He'd grinned at them and said, "I'll be home in a week, two weeks at the most, with a paycheck. Maybe I can talk them into giving me an advance, so I can get some money to you sooner than that. You kids'll be okay for that long. We'll go out and celebrate. Steaks, maybe."

"Or pizza." Buddy had offered a counter suggestion, and he'd laughed and hugged her.

"Whatever you want, little Buddy. You mind what Bart says, now. No squabbling, okay?"

And he'd gotten into the car with Rich Painter, to drive over to Lewiston, where they'd both gotten jobs. They felt good about it, because he'd only be gone a short time, and it was a relief that someone had hired him after the mill shut down and practically everybody in town got laid off. There wouldn't be any more work here at home, and they'd probably have to move, but that was okay, as long as they were together. It was lucky Dad had had truck driving experience, even though he hadn't liked being away from home so much, which was why he'd quit to go into the mill. That way he could be home every night even if it was hard, monotonous work.

Only that had been well over a week ago, almost two weeks, and there had been no word from Dad. No money order, no postcard, no phone call. Nothing.

Buddy closed the lid on another box and tried to stop sniveling. She didn't want to make it any harder on Bart than it already was.

They lugged all the boxes out to the garage, and Buddy prayed Dad would return soon and find them another place to live.

They left the house after they'd fixed a last meal—canned tamales and peaches—on Thursday night. It was a good thing Bart had his driver's license, so nobody could stop them from taking the car through town.

They had trouble finding a parking spot near the bus station at first, so they pulled in a couple of blocks down. There was a theater across the street, and Buddy suggested maybe they should go to the movie until the traffic cleared out and they could get closer to the bus station.

"I don't think we'd better," Bart said soberly. "Dad gave me enough money to last until he came home, but he's late. We don't know how long what I have left will have to last. I can't get at his bank account, and I don't think there's much in it, anyway. You brought a book, didn't you, Buddy? We'd better just sit and read until it gets dark."

Buddy tried, but she couldn't concentrate. She opened a box of crackers, and they shared them. After a while traffic thinned out, and they drove by the station again. This time Bart found a spot just half a block down.

They arranged their pillows and blankets as comfortably as they could and tried to settle down and sleep. It wasn't late, but it had been an exhausting day, especially emotionally. For Bart's sake, Buddy tried not to cry out loud.

She didn't successfully muffle her sobs, though, because he reached over the back of the seat and squeezed her shoulder comfortingly. "It'll be okay," he assured her. "This won't last for long."

When you cry, your nose gets plugged up and you can't breathe well enough to sleep lying down. Buddy thought longingly of her bed—her *rented* bed, she remembered, no longer hers—and squirmed around trying to get more comfortable.

Would it have been different if they'd had their own furniture, the things they'd had before Mama died? When they moved that last time, after she was gone, their father hadn't seemed to want to keep anything that reminded him she wasn't there. So they had sold what they had and rented the furnished house. Had that been a mistake?

A police car went by, siren screaming, as she was trying to say her prayers. The neon lights of a bar across the street blinked off and on, making reflections on the metallic door handle. A stray cat meowed piteously, setting off a fresh gush of tears. *I understand how you feel, kitty,* she told it silently. *Nowhere to go, not knowing where your next meal is coming from.*

About that time Buddy realized that she had to stop feeling sorry for herself. She could almost hear Mama's voice. "Having a little pity-party, are we, Buddy?"

Defensively, she thought, *Well, who's more entitled to one?* But that made her feel guilty. She *did* know where her next meal was coming from. They still had some groceries left, in a box in the trunk. They could eat tuna, and pork and beans, and peaches right out of the cans. For a few days yet. Dad would surely be back by then. And Bart wasn't whining and feeling sorry for himself.

In the backseat her brother shifted position, trying to arrange his tall frame on the too-short seat.

"Bart?" Buddy murmured. "What are we going to do if Dad doesn't come back really soon?"

"I don't know," Bart said. "Don't worry about it, Buddy. I'll think of something."

She finally fell asleep, wondering if her back and neck would be broken before morning.

It must have been several hours later when she woke in a panic. Someone was trying to open the door on the sidewalk side of the car.

Buddy reared up, gasping in alarm, and saw the face pressed against the window. A man with a big nose stared in at her, his bad skin tinted by the light from the neon sign across the street. She struggled to a sitting position, drawing as far away from him as she could get.

Behind her, Bart reared up also and rapped sharply on his own window. "Get out of here! Leave us alone!" he commanded, and the face retreated. "It's just a drunk," he said. "The doors are locked. He can't get in."

Buddy watched the man wander away, unable to walk steadily. He had frightened Buddy badly, and she resented his peering in at them. But a part of her recognized that he, too, was without a home. "We can't keep parking here," she said, her voice shaking.

"No," Bart agreed, leaning back into his pillow. He twisted around and held his watch up so he could read it in the reddish light. "It's only an hour or so until daylight. Go back to sleep, Buddy.

We're safe enough as long as we don't unlock the doors."

She didn't feel safe. She wouldn't feel safe again until Dad came back, and they were living in a house again.

As soon as it was light, they went into the bus station. They didn't need to get dressed, because they'd slept in their clothes, but they had to use the rest rooms. Nobody paid any attention or seemed to care if they washed their faces there and brushed their teeth.

Back in the car, Buddy was too depressed to ask her brother any questions. He waited until they'd eaten a crackers and peanut butter breakfast, washed down with canned juice, before he told her what he'd decided.

"While we were in the station I asked about the price of a ticket to Haysville." When she opened her mouth to protest, he put his hand over it. "No, don't argue, Buddy. I thought about it all night long, and we don't have any choice. I can't keep you out of school, and I can't let you live in a car, not even for another night. I called Aunt Cassie. She said of course they'd take you in, so I'm putting you on a bus today. There's one that leaves early this morning."

She shoved his hand aside in indignation. "And what about you, then? Aren't you coming, too?"

"I can't," Bart said, and his tone sobered her.

"It's been too long, Buddy. Dad thought he'd be back by now. He'd have come home if he could have. And if he could have called, he would have. Something's happened to him, and I have to go find out what."

She swallowed, her fighting spirit wilting. "What could have happened?" she whispered. "You don't think he's . . . hurt or something, do you?" *Or dead?* she was wondering.

Bart inhaled deeply and then let the breath all out. "Maybe. It had to be something serious, or he'd have kept his promise to get in touch. I have to go, Buddy. Don't make it any harder by refusing to cooperate. You have to go to Aunt Cassie's."

The recollection of that drunken man peering into the car while he tried the door handle sent a shudder through her, and she knew Bart was right. But she made one last feeble try to avoid being sent to an aunt who had, it had always seemed, not liked their mother. "Why can't I come with you, then, wherever you have to go?"

"Because you're eleven years old, not seventeen, and we'd still have to be living in the car until I either find Dad or get a job to earn enough to support us. I don't want us to be apart, either, kid, so don't make it any harder than it has to be."

Her shoulders sagged, and she held back the prickle of tears. "Okay," she said softly. "What time's the bus?"

# 2

It rained all the way to Haysville. The drops on the bus window beside her seemed like the tears Buddy didn't want to show to the other passengers.

A middle-aged lady boarded at the last stop before Buddy's destination. She looked over the other people who nearly filled the bus and dropped into the seat beside Buddy with a smile Buddy had trouble returning. As the bus crossed the state line, clueing her in that she didn't have too much longer to ride, the woman opened a paper bag and started taking out her lunch.

To Buddy's embarrassment, her stomach growled. The lady looked at Buddy, and her smile widened. "My daughter fixed me far more than I'm going to be able to eat. Would you like to share?" She opened a plastic bag and held it up to sniff at it.

"This sandwich is tuna. There's also a . . . ham and cheese, I think. I'm sort of partial to tuna salad. How about you eating this one? Unless you don't like ham and cheese, of course."

Buddy suspected the woman was offering the one she thought Buddy would prefer, and her stomach was too empty to refuse. "Thank you," Buddy said, and accepted the sandwich.

It was a really good one. Mama used to say that being half-starved makes all food taste better, and Buddy believed it.

"Going home, are you?" the woman asked in a friendly manner.

There was no way Buddy was going to try to explain. "Visiting my relatives in Haysville," she managed.

"Oh, that's good. My goodness! Sharon packed a candy bar in here. I hardly ever eat chocolate. Ah, there are some peppermints. I like those better. Here, you take the chocolate."

She didn't refuse that, either. Bart had given her a few dollars for an emergency, but she hadn't wanted to spend any of it on food when they made a rest stop. Buddy let the chocolate melt slowly on her tongue, savoring every bit of it.

*If I'd wanted to take this trip, I'd probably have enjoyed the scenery,* she thought. The leaves were turning color, all different shades of yellow and deep gold, and an occasional splash of brilliant red. Mama had always said that fall was the nicest time of year, especially in Montana. It was hard to get excited about fall color when you didn't have a home that belonged to you, though.

The rain stopped just as they approached Haysville. POPULATION 3,023, the sign said. Buddy had enjoyed coming here when they were a whole family, but that hadn't happened often, and never since before her mother died. She took a close look as the bus began to slow.

The highway was the main street of town, and the businesses were scattered out along about six or eight blocks, with houses on side streets. The first thing she noticed was how many of the stores were closed. She spotted the Ostrom Appliance and Hardware store, and it, too, was locked up and empty. Buddy wondered if Grandpa Harry Ostrom had died since she'd been here. If so, no one had told them.

Grass growing in the cracks of the sidewalk, and debris lay against the walls of the buildings. Hardly anybody was walking on the street, so it was easy to spot Aunt Cassie when the bus pulled over to the curb. There wasn't even a bus station, just a little sign that signified the bus would stop there.

Buddy was the only one getting out, except for the driver, who had to unload her suitcase from underneath the bus. Aunt Cassie looked pretty much as Buddy remembered her, maybe a little heavier. She was wearing a print housedress and a red sweater, and she came forward with a smile. "Buddy! How nice to see you after all this time!" She gave Buddy a hug. She smelled nice, like fresh-baked bread. "I hope you had a good trip."

It wasn't exactly a question, and Buddy didn't feel the need to answer. How could it be a good trip under these circumstances?

"It's only a couple of blocks to walk," Cassie said, and reached for the suitcase. "I'll carry this until I get tired, and then you can take a turn."

They went up one of the side streets, which were wide and lined with shrubs and trees. Most of the houses were separated by good-sized lawns, now turning dry after a hot summer, and Buddy recognized the Ostrom house as they approached it. Mama and her sisters had grown up there, and it was in the background of a lot of the early snap-shots. It seemed strange to think of Mama having lived all her life in this one house before her marriage. Buddy's own family had lived in at least a half a dozen houses that she could remember.

It was a big old two-story house with a covered veranda on three sides of it. There was a porch swing, and wicker chairs with faded flowered cushions.

"Everybody here is just fine," Aunt Cassie said as they turned in, just as if Buddy had asked about them.

A curtain twitched in one of the windows, and

Buddy quickly glanced that way, but it immediately fell back into place, and she couldn't tell who'd been looking out. Mr. Beaman had said the thing to do was go to their relatives, but it didn't feel right. It didn't feel as if she were joining family, but strangers whose pictures she'd only seen in snapshots.

After all, they'd stopped writing after Mama died, before she'd died, actually. There had been some kind of misunderstanding, some reason why Aunt Addie, especially, hadn't been friendly with Mama. It was, Buddy thought, a reason that had kept them from frequent visits to Mama's hometown. "Since Mother died, they don't exactly make me feel welcome," Mama had said before that last visit, "but I want some of my things that are still stored there, so I'm going."

And, after that, none of them had ever visited again. Buddy tried not to think about it. She wasn't sure she was really welcome, either.

They went in the front door, and Aunt Cassie set the suitcase down at the foot of the stairs in the front hallway. Then she led the way through a dining room with old-fashioned furniture into a big kitchen that smelled of the fresh-baked bread set out on a counter and of soup simmering on an old black woodstove. There was an electric stove, too, right beside the black one, which seemed peculiar.

"She's here!" Aunt Cassie sang out. "Come and say hello!"

Aunt Addie appeared from a pantry, wiping her hands on a towel. "Welcome, Amy Kate," she said.

Hardly anybody ever called her by her real name. Aunt Cassie laughed. "Oh, she's Buddy, don't you remember that?"

From the look on Addie's face, it was clear she thought Buddy was a stupid name for a girl, though she didn't say so. "I thought maybe your brother would come with you," she noted.

Buddy's throat was dry. "No. He . . . he had to look for Daddy."

Addie's expression sharpened. "Something happen to Dan, did it?"

"We don't know for sure, but when he took the new job he said he'd be back in a week, and we haven't heard from him," Buddy said.

Addie got a pinched look around her mouth, as if Buddy had said something unpleasant.

At the same time, Cassie said, "Don't you remember? I told you that. Grandpa, come and meet Buddy. Do you remember her? EllaBelle's girl?"

The old man who emerged from a bedroom off the kitchen was still tall and thin, but no longer elegant. He leaned heavily on a cane and looked at the newcomer with faded blue eyes. "EllaBelle?"

"Sure. You remember her. Our little sister."

"Sister," the old man echoed. "Hello, Sister."

Cassie smiled and patted him on the arm. "Always called all of us 'Sister,' didn't you, Grandpa? Couldn't remember our names, even when we were little girls, so we were all 'Sister.' I'll bet everybody's ready for lunch, aren't they?" She raised her voice. "Max! Lunchtime!"

Who was Max? Buddy didn't remember anyone named Max.

"Did I have lunch yet?" Grandpa asked uncertainly.

"No, dear, we're all going to eat in just a moment," Cassie assured him. "We waited for Buddy. Max! Don't hold us up!"

The boy who came from a rear hallway was carrying a kitten, which he lowered to the floor. "You told me to bring in some firewood, remember? Look what I found. Can I keep him?"

Buddy guessed Max to be somewhere near her own age, though he was a head taller.

Addie spoke sharply. "You know Gus doesn't like cats." That was the clue. Buddy remembered that Cassie was married to Uncle Gus. There were no pictures of him in the photo album. Buddy hadn't known he had a son. Max couldn't be Cassie's son, because she and Gus had only married just before Mama died. Cassie's stepson, then.

"I could give him some milk," Max said, and went to the cupboard for a small bowl.

"Actually," Addie said, "too much milk is not all that good for a cat."

"He hasn't had too much of anything," Max stated. "You can feel his ribs sticking out."

"Say hello to your cousin Buddy," Cassie said, putting dishes on the big, round table.

Max looked at her. "Hi," he said. "We're not really cousins, of course."

*He would be rather nice-looking,* Buddy thought, *if he smiled instead of being so poker-faced.*

He bent to pour milk into the bowl, then nudged the kitten toward it. The scruffy little gray-and-white creature drank greedily.

"Grandpa, did you wash your hands?" Cassie was asking now. "Do you want me to help you?"

Why would a grown man need help washing his hands? Cassie turned away and headed toward the bathroom off the back hallway, steering the old man ahead of her. Aunt Addie was busy slicing bread, and Max and Buddy were left standing there.

"I always wanted a kitten," Buddy said.

"Somebody didn't want him. They dumped him off to shift for himself," Max said. And then he shifted his attention from the kitten to her again. "I doubt if you're going to like it here very much. Everybody in this house is crazy."

Buddy blinked. "I beg your pardon?" she said, startled.

"It's a very dysfunctional family," he told her. "Unless you're a fruitcake, too, you probably won't fit in very well."

If this was his idea of a welcome, Buddy didn't think she could expect much of Max. She thought she had a general idea of what *dysfunctional* meant, but she missed having Bart there to explain so she'd know for sure. Her brother never made fun of her when she didn't understand something.

Buddy swallowed. "I don't expect to be here for long. Just until Bart finds Dad." Her heart was beating very fast. If she'd hoped for a moment that the only other person her age in this household might be a friend, that hope was fading.

Max looked her full in the face then. "Your old man abandon you, did he?"

Indignation surged through her. "No! He left town with a friend for a new job, after he got laid off at the mill. When it closed, practically everybody in town was out of work. Most of the men had to go somewhere else to look for jobs."

"That's what he told you, huh?" Clearly Max didn't believe her, and it stirred Buddy's anger.

"That's what he told us, because it was the truth. He'd never abandon us."

"But he went away and didn't come back, huh?" Max's mouth slid into a sneer. "My old man lies all the time, too."

"Mine doesn't!" Buddy snapped. "He hasn't come back because something happened to him, so he couldn't! My brother Bart's gone to find out what it was!"

Max shrugged. "Good luck," he said, but she could tell he didn't believe her, didn't mean it.

"Now, Grandpa," Aunt Cassie was saying as they returned to the room, "you sit right down, and I'll dish up the soup. Beef and barley vegetable, it is. You like that, remember?"

Grandpa hesitated in the middle of the room. "Where do you want me to sit?"

"Right there on the end, same as always," Cassie said, guiding him with a touch on his elbow. She picked up a bowl and a big ladle. "You can sit right there beside him, Buddy."

Hesitantly, Buddy obeyed, wondering why Grandpa, who lived here, didn't know where to sit. And why he had to be reminded that he liked beef and barley vegetable soup. It didn't seem the sort of thing a person was likely to forget.

The others took their places around the big, round table while Cassie placed steaming, wonderful-smelling soup in front of them. There were thick slices of bread, too, on a plate right in front of Grandpa.

Cassie sat down on the other side of Grandpa and buttered him a slice of bread, cutting it in half as she placed it on his plate. "Would you like to ask the blessing, Grandpa?" she asked.

Awkwardly, Buddy bowed her head with the others. They'd always said grace before meals when Mama was alive. Sometimes Dad remembered, sometimes not. They'd almost gotten out of the habit, though Buddy felt guilty enough so that she prayed silently.

"Thank you, Lord, for all your blessings, and for our food. And if Sister made pie for dessert, we thank you for that, too. Amen."

Buddy started to smile at that last part, until she saw that no one else was smiling except Aunt Cassie.

"No pie today, Grandpa," Cassie told him gently. "Oatmeal cookies."

The old man reached up to a small device hanging on a cord around his neck and pressed it. A female voice said, "The time is 1:03 P.M."

"Time to eat," Grandpa said, and picked up his spoon.

Everybody else dug in, too. The soup was marvelous, rich and thick and meaty. So was the homemade bread.

"Is there any jam?" Grandpa asked.

There was a small jar beside his plate. Buddy looked from Grandpa to Aunt Cassie, who met her gaze sadly as she pushed the jar closer to the old man's hand. "Right here, Grandpa." Then, to Buddy, she added, "He has macular degeneration. He can't see things that are directly in front of him."

Buddy must have looked bewildered. Across the table from her, Max saw that she was confused, and made his own explanation. "That means that he has peripheral vision—you know, around the edges, he can see light and color—but in the middle of his sight, where your face would be if he could see it, it's just a black spot. He's been legally blind for the past two years."

Blind? Now she understood why Cassie had guided him to the bathroom and his chair, why he needed help washing up, and why he wore a speaking timepiece around his neck. Grandpa Harry's eyes looked perfectly normal, she thought, but they could no longer see the way they used to.

Buddy dug into the lunch, hungry in spite of what she'd eaten on the bus. The soup and fresh bread were delicious, and she said so. Cassie smiled her appreciation of the compliment. "You want to get the cookies, dear? They're on a plate right over there."

Buddy wondered what Bart was eating, or if he was eating at all. He did have money, but not very much, and he needed to pay for gas. All he'd known was the name of the town where Dad and Rich Painter had gone for the promised jobs. Dad had told them the name of the trucking company that had agreed to hire them, but neither of them had remembered what it was.

Whenever she thought of it, which was practically

all the time, Buddy prayed that her brother would be able to find Dad, and that he was all right.

They were finishing the cookies—Buddy ate three, the same as Grandpa—when the doorbell rang in the front of the house. Max, stuffing his fourth cookie into his mouth, pushed back his chair. "I'll get it," he said. "It's probably Hank. He said he'd come over and we'd go ride bikes for a while."

They heard boys' voices, and then Max came back with a handful of envelopes, putting them down beside Addie's plate. "Mail's here. There's a manuscript returned for you, Addie"—he plunked down a large manila envelope—"and a letter from Gordon. Plus the electric bill."

Gordon, Buddy knew, was the only boy in the family, between Addie and Cassie in age, all of them older than her mother had been. He was the only one besides her mother who had moved away from Haysville; he had left before Buddy was even born. He lived in Los Angeles, where he was a successful attorney.

Addie picked up the envelope, held it to the light, tore it open, then made a small grunting sound of annoyance. "I don't have my glasses. I left them on my dresser. Fetch them for me, Max."

"Don't have time, the guys are waiting," Max said, and fled after grabbing another handful of cookies.

Addie looked after him in exasperation. "His

legs are younger than mine. Why can't he do me a favor?" she asked of no one in particular.

"My legs are young, too," Buddy said impulsively. "Could I get your glasses?"

"Yes, please. Top of the stairs, the first room on the right. They're on the dresser. You might as well take this up, too, and leave it." She handed Buddy the big, thick manila envelope without opening it.

The spectacles were right where Addie had said they were. Buddy picked them up before she noticed the dark red leather-covered photograph album on the nightstand a few feet away.

It looked just like the one Mama had left. Buddy couldn't have said why she paused to open it, except that perhaps she hoped there would be pictures of her mother there.

There were a number of them, some that Buddy had never seen before. The ones in the front of the book were old, when the sisters were little girls, and then there were snapshots taken as they grew into their teens.

Buddy stopped flipping the pages, realizing that she was intruding on Addie's private things. The pages flopped back into place, but not before a loose, enlarged snapshot fell out onto the old-fashioned floral rug.

Automatically, Buddy stooped to pick it up and then stopped.

The picture had been taken in front of this very house, many years ago. She recognized Addie, looking young and happy, but that wasn't the surprising part. She was standing with her arm around a young man who was also laughing, and he had his arm around her, too.

The man was Buddy's father.

She stared, stupified.

Dad and Aunt Addie? Hugging each other?

She brought the picture closer to her eyes to examine it more carefully.

There was no question that the young man was Dan Adams. He was almost a dead ringer for Bart, taken when he was maybe only a few years older than Bart was now.

The voice from below drifted up the stairway. "Can't you find them, Buddy? On the dresser, just inside the door."

Buddy jerked, jabbed the picture into the photo album, and spun toward the doorway. "I found them," she called, and started downstairs. She had no idea why her father had been hugging Aunt Addie. It made her most uncomfortable as she descended to the ground floor and handed over Addie's glasses. Somehow she felt it was important, though she didn't know why.

# 3

At home Buddy had often helped her father with the cooking, and she was expected to clear the table and help with the dishes. Uncertain if she should offer or simply start picking up the bowls, she hesitated as Addie settled her glasses on her nose and began to read.

Cassie waited, too. "Did he send a check?"

"Umm. Yes, right here." Addie paused in her reading long enough to fish the check out of the envelope. "He's not coming home for Grandpa's birthday party, though. He's too busy."

Cassie's face fell. "It's not every day a person gets to be ninety-two. I thought it would be nice if Gordon came home for the party."

"What party?" Grandpa Harry asked.

"Your birthday party, honey," Cassie said, leaning

toward him and raising her voice slightly. "On the seventeenth."

"I'm having a party? How old am I?'

"Ninety-two," Cassie repeated.

"According to the Bible, a person's years are three score and ten. Isn't that seventy years?"

"Yes, but some live longer, and some live less. Grandma lived to be eighty, remember?"

*And Mama had died at thirty-eight,* Buddy thought. It was hard to figure out why some died so young, and others lived to be so old.

Cassie stood up and reached for the nearest bowls, and Buddy moved to help her.

"Oh, thank you, dear. Just rinse them in the sink, there, and put them in the dishwasher. This way."

"We never had a dishwasher," Buddy said, obeying orders. "I usually wash the dishes."

"I do most of the cooking, so Addie used to do most of the dishwashing, until she bullied Gordon into buying us a dishwasher," Cassie stated.

Addie was distracted from her letter. "Well, he never does anything else for this family, does he? Grandpa's *his* relative as well as ours. There's no reason he shouldn't pitch in and do his share, even if it's only with money for things we can use."

Grandpa pushed the button on the talking watch, which squawked a response. "The time is 1:47 P.M." He stood up, unhooked his cane from the back of his chair, and headed toward the bedroom that opened off the kitchen. "It's time for my nap," he said to nobody in particular.

It hadn't taken long to load the dishwasher, and Cassie smiled at Buddy. "I guess we'd better get you settled, hadn't we? If you were going to stay for a while, we'd clear out that back bedroom upstairs. But it's got an awful lot of junk in it, and we figured since you'll probably be back with the rest of your family within a few days, maybe you wouldn't mind sleeping in the little sewing room. It has stuff stored in it, too, but it's not like upstairs."

Again Addie put down her letter to comment. "What makes you think she's only going to be here for a few days? They don't know where Dan is, do they? Or if he's even coming back?"

"Of course he's coming back," Buddy said quickly, shocked.

"He never was very responsible," Addie asserted, to Buddy's further indignation. "Always doing things on the spur of the moment, without thinking of the consequences."

Buddy bit her lower lip. That wasn't the way she thought of her father at all, but in Addie's house it probably wasn't polite to say so.

"That was a long time ago," Cassie said soothingly. "I'm sure he's changed since then. Come along, Buddy, and we'll get you fixed up."

"It's Friday. School's still open. Somebody should take her over and sign her up," Addie said.

"School?" Buddy couldn't keep still for that. "Aunt Cassie's right. I'll probably only be here a few days. There's no need to go to school for that little time."

"Nobody knows for sure, do they?" Addie asked. "The law says kids have to go to school, and there's no reason to get behind."

"All right, just in case Dan and Bart don't show up by the first of the week, you can take her over and talk to Herbert," Cassie said. "After we get her squared away in the sewing room. Max could do it, but those seventh graders are off for a couple of days, I guess, so you'll have to do it."

She led the way, and Buddy followed, disturbed by everybody else being in control and making decisions for her. "Who's Herbert?" she asked, pausing in the doorway of the small room opening off the dining room.

"He's the school principal. We went to school with him, years ago. Was a friend of Gordon's, actually. They both went away to college the same year. Gordon never came back home to live, always felt this was a hayseed town with no future. But Herbert's parents wanted him to come home to work as a teacher, and finally enough people died off, so he got to be principal. Here, let's put your suitcase on this chair. You can just leave it there and take your things out as you need them, if you want to. Or if it turns out you're here longer, I think there are a couple of empty drawers in that chest. The daybed's all made up for you. There's an extra blanket right here."

The room was very small, and crowded with cardboard cartons as well as a sewing machine. But no drunks could peek in the windows at her, and there was a bathroom just a few doors away. She'd be in a house, not a car. She didn't know if this kept her from being homeless or not, but she'd *feel* homeless until Dad and Bart came and got her.

"Thank you," Buddy said, swallowing around the lump in her throat. She hoped Addie wasn't right about her being here indefinitely.

Addie came to the doorway, putting her letter back into its envelope. "There's an extra twenty-five dollars in here to buy a present for Grandpa's birthday," she said. "Where on earth does he think we're going to be able to shop? Why couldn't he have bought a gift himself, in that big city, where they have hundreds of stores to choose from? He lived here all his life until he graduated from high school. He must remember the nearest decent-sized town is sixty miles away."

"Maybe you should have suggested some-thing specific as a present," Cassie said. "The way you usually tell him what we need or want? Gordon's pretty reasonable about getting things when you do."

"Why do I have to think of things like that? Hasn't he got a brain of his own?" Addie said crossly. "We've got enough to do right here, keeping up this old barn of a house. Worrying about an old man who has to have everything done for him. Can't leave him alone for fear of what he'll do. Can't go anyplace unless we take him, and he doesn't want to go anywhere but church, and then he embarrasses us by his loud belching and singing so loud, he drowns out the organ."

"Everybody there has known him all their lives, and they're used to him. We're living here, so we'd have to keep house, anyway," Cassie said. "And where do you want to go, Addie? We'd be practically hermits whether we had Grandpa to look after or not."

"We're too young to be hermits," Addie snapped. "And I'd like the option of having some choices, not having to do it because we're stuck with taking care of him."

Cassie was beginning to seem a bit annoyed herself. "Well, then, go ahead and go somewhere. We'll still be here, Gus and Max and I."

"Gus!" Addie let out a gust of air. "Fat lot of use *he* is. Spends every minute down at the Hayloft with the rest of those bums."

"He can't work, Addie. You know how bad his back is. You can't expect the man to sit around the house with a couple of women who are too busy to even talk to him."

"He can't talk about anything but football and basketball and baseball scores, anyway. I never did figure out why you married him, Cassie."

Buddy, feeling as if she was unwillingly listening to a conversation that was none of her business, shifted her weight from one foot to the other, trapped inside the small room until they finished what they were saying.

Cassie responded quietly, sounding hurt. "Same reason you married Ed, I suppose. I never had a chance to get out of this little town and meet anybody else, getting close to forty and it didn't look like I was ever going to get a chance to find anyone better. He promised me he was going to quit drinking, and Max needed more of a home than the two of them had, living in that little apartment. I thought we could all be a family."

Addie's face flushed, and Buddy wondered how many times they'd already had this same conversation.

"At least Ed had the decency to die on me," Addie said flatly. "I don't have to lie awake at night, listening to him fumbling with the key to get in. Listen, Buddy, it's not raining, so let's walk over to the school and get you registered. It's too late for you to stay today, but you can go on Monday. Max can show you around."

Buddy had her doubts that Max was going to want to do anything of the sort. Yet going with Addie seemed the only way to end this mortifying eavesdropping on what should have been a private conversation. Funny, that they could be embarrassed by Grandpa's behavior, yet not be aware of their own.

Under other circumstances, if she'd been with her own family, for instance, Buddy might have enjoyed the walk through Haysville. It was a pretty time of year, and now that the sun had come out, the red and gold leaves brightened the lawns and yards everywhere. There were lots of interesting-looking houses, all of them old, the kind that Mama had always said she'd like to have someday. They looked friendly, and comfortable, even if quite a few of them could have benefited from a coat of paint or some fence repairs.

The school looked like something out of an old movie. Red brick, and there was an odd tube coming out of the side of it from the second story.

"What's that thing?" Buddy asked, breaking the silence that had held between them all the way here.

"Fire escape," Addie told her. "We used to love fire drills when we were kids. We got to open the door at the top and slide down. EllaBelle got in trouble once when she and Nicky Welton came down it without permission when there wasn't a drill."

As they walked up the front walk, Buddy inspected her aunt more closely. "You must know lots of things about my mother that I never heard."

"Of course, she was my sister. I had to baby-sit her when she was really little. The last spanking I ever got was when I was supposed to be watching her, but I was reading a book and didn't notice that she'd disappeared. My mother came home and demanded to know where she was, and I said I didn't know and I didn't care."

"What if she'd been hurt?" Buddy asked, shocked.

"Well, I was pretty sure she hadn't been. There was no traffic on this street, even back then, before this was the dead town it is now. And everybody knew her and where to bring her home. It wasn't the last time I had to baby-sit her, but I never again made the mistake of saying I didn't care. Mom used to make us pick our own switches off that willow tree in the backyard, and if we didn't bring her one that was strong enough, she'd make us get another, tougher one, and use it longer. My legs stung like crazy when she got through with me."

"Mama never mentioned getting switched," Buddy said as they reached the front door.

"I don't know if *she* ever did. She was the baby, and she was the favorite. She got away with every-thing Cassie and Gordon and I never got away with." Addie pulled open the door and urged Buddy in ahead of her. "She was a spoiled brat, actually."

That didn't fit with Buddy's recollections of her mother, either. But there was no time to pursue it. A sign over a doorway to their left said, OFFICE, and that was where they were headed.

The school looked and smelled old.

"Is this the elementary school?" Buddy asked. "Or the middle school?"

"This is everything from kindergarten through twelfth grade. Hi, Sylvia," Addie addressed the elderly lady at the front desk. "We need to see Herbert to enroll my niece for . . . what grade, Buddy? Sixth?"

Buddy nodded unwillingly.

Sylvia didn't have a nice, modern telephone system where she could push a button to summer her superior. Instead, she turned her head and called through the open doorway behind her, "Mr. Faulkner, Addie Ostrom wants to see you."

The man who emerged to greet them and usher them into his tiny cubicle looked older than Addie, mostly because he was nearly bald. He had leather patches on the elbows of his tweed jacket. "Well, your niece, you say? EllaBelle's girl, is she?"

"Buddy Adams," Buddy said.

He blinked. "They always call you Buddy?"

"In school they call me Amy Kate," Buddy said. "It's mostly my dad who calls me Buddy." It was beginning to get embarrassing. Everybody reacted the same way to that silly nickname; they thought it was stupid.

Herbert Faulker nodded, as if Amy Kate was a more acceptable name. "Sixth grade, eh? That would be Mrs. Hope's class. Fifth and sixth grade. You bring your transcripts with you?"

Buddy wasn't sure what *transcripts* were, but she was sure she didn't have them.

"She wasn't expecting to have to go to school," Addie said. "Something happened to her dad— you remember Dan Adams, don't you?—and she doesn't have any papers. But we don't know how long she'll be with us, so we thought we should sign her up."

Herbert pursed his lips. "I can't sign up somebody with no transcripts. Where did you come from, Amy Kate? Where did you go to school last?"

She told him, squirming a bit on the hard chair she'd been offered. "The mill closed, and everybody was out of work, so my dad went with a friend to Lewiston. They'd been offered jobs there. Only he hasn't come back yet, and my brother went to look for him. They'll probably come and get me in a few days."

His eyebrows rose. "But you don't know for sure? Well, you ought to be in school, of course. We'll have to write to your old school and find out where to put you."

"She just told you where to put her. She's in the sixth grade."

"But she has to have the transcripts from her last school," Herbert said, frowning ever so slightly.

Addie had no more patience with the school principal than she'd had with Grandpa or Aunt Cassie. "Oh, come on, Herbert. You always were a stickler for protocol, but you never had any common sense. You were a wimpy little boy and you're a wimpy man. Put her into the sixth-grade class and then send for whatever papers you need. What difference does a few days make?"

The man had gone from pink to red to near purple at her words. "There are rules and regulations, Addie. I don't make them, I'm just expected to follow them—"

Addie made a rude noise. "If the rule said you couldn't leave a burning building before the fire truck arrived, you'd stand there and fry off the rest of your hair. Buddy'll be here at nine o'clock on Monday morning. Do you want Sylvia to get the basic information now, or then?"

The purple countenance was fading only a

little. "Now, I suppose," he said reluctantly. "But I hope you understand, Addie, that—"

Addie stood up, pulling Buddy with her. "You want me to talk to Sam Bass and the rest of the school board? See if they're all as nervous Nellies as you are? Sam's no mental giant, but he's got the interests of the kids at heart. I can't think he'd keep a kid out of school just because she's homeless at the moment, and isn't carrying the proper documentation. God only knows when Dan will show up, if he ever does. You must remember how unreliable he was when he made a promise."

Buddy felt color warming her own face at being pronounced *homeless*. And why did Addie have to keep making slighting remarks about her father? It was obvious that the school principal, too, was struggling with rage as well as humiliation. Yet he made one more attempt to temper Addie's attack.

"I only recollect one promise he made that he didn't keep, Addie, and it was nothing like these circumstances. I'm sure he'll be back for his little girl as soon as he can. But you're right: Until he comes, she needs to be in school. Don't worry, Amy Kate, I'll get in touch with your last school, and we'll get this all straightened out. You go talk to Sylvia, now, and she can get the basic information."

Sylvia was perfectly kind. She filled out a couple of forms, and Buddy felt her embarrassment diminishing. Still, being designated as *homeless* and hearing that her father was considered unreliable and untrustworthy was very upsetting.

She didn't say a single word to Addie all the way home.

# 4

The house was filled with the mouthwatering aroma of roasting meat. Addie went upstairs to take off her sweater without any suggestions as to what Buddy should do next. There was no sign of Cassie or Grandpa, so she wandered out the back door to the rear yard. It was a pleasant place, with plastic lawn chairs under the brilliantly colored trees, and a round table that still had puddles of water on it.

But there was nothing to do there. She walked around for a few minutes, looking at the remains of a large garden and wondering who tended it, then went back inside.

She wished desperately that Bart had come with her. Or that he'd call and tell her he'd found Dad. He *had* to be all right, didn't he?

But things did happen to people. There had been that terrible accident that had killed her mother, when her car had slid on the ice and crashed. Everybody had said EllaBelle Adams must have died instantly when she hit the cement wall, that she couldn't have felt any pain.

Buddy hadn't even been able to see her at the last. They'd closed the casket. Not that she wanted to see what had happened to her mother; yet for the longest time she had felt that Mama hadn't really died, that she was still alive somewhere, and would come walking through the door any minute.

But an accident wouldn't have happened to Dad. He was a good driver. He'd only given up driving trucks, which he loved, to work in the mill after Mama died, so she and Bart wouldn't be home alone so much. He said it was the other fellow you had to look out for, the one who *wasn't* a good, careful driver. And he would have been driving a truck, and sitting up above other drivers, and not very likely to be injured even if there was an accident. He'd told her that, so she wouldn't worry.

It was impossible not to worry, though. What if even her brother didn't come back? What if she never found out what had happened to either of them? What if she had to stay here with Aunt Addie and Aunt Cassie forever?

Her eyes prickled and her throat ached, thinking about it.

The screen door slammed behind her, and she spun around. Max was standing at the top of the steps. "What happened to my kitten?" he demanded.

"What?" Buddy couldn't imagine why he was asking *her*.

"Are you deaf? I asked what happened to my kitten?"

"I heard you," she said with as much dignity as she could muster. "I just didn't understand why you'd think *I* would know. I haven't seen him."

"I put him in that box just inside the back door."

"I guess he must have climbed out. I don't know where he went." And then, because she would have made the offer to anyone else, she added, "Do you want me to help you look for him?"

"He's too little to climb out. Somebody must have taken him out."

"Well, it wasn't me."

Max was scowling. "I heard you went over to sign up for school. Does that mean you're going to stay here?"

It only occurred to her at that moment that Max was school age. "I hope not, but they said I should go as long as I'm here," she said. "How come you weren't in school this afternoon?"

"The seventh graders are off until Monday. They're fumigating our room and the library, right next door to it, and there was nowhere for us to have classes."

"Fumigating?" Buddy echoed.

"Yes. Some guys came in to clean up the mess and the smell and stuff." Max's scowl had faded. "We had an incident yesterday. Somebody brought in a skunk, and it got loose. Old Faulkner thinks the rooms are going to be fit to move back into by Monday, but nobody else thinks so. You ever smelled skunk up close?"

"Yes," Buddy admitted. "Our neighbor's dog tangled with one once. They didn't let him into the house for a week, even after they washed him in tomato juice. He still stunk."

"Exactly," Max said with satisfaction. "I'm betting it'll still stink on Monday. I brought my books and my backpack home, and I can still smell it on them. And the skunk wasn't actually anywhere near *me*. Cassie said I had to leave them on the back porch to air out, but they're no better yet."

"What happened to the person who brought in the skunk? How did he get it?"

"Trapped it in a box in his backyard. I don't know yet. He'd probably have been expelled, but his dad's head of the school board. They almost kicked me out of school once for bringing a mouse in my shirt pocket. You don't have much clout when your dad's the town drunk."

"Is he?" Buddy asked, shocked.

"Yeah. Well, he's not the only one. But he's no-body the town would elect to the school board. Poor Cassie believed him when he said he'd stop drinking, but he's a liar, too."

"But they didn't actually expel you?"

Max snorted. "No. Not after Addie went over and gave old Faulker a tongue-lashing. You know, I think he's afraid of her. I think he was afraid of her when he was a kid and he and Gordon got into trouble, and she bailed *them* out. Afterward she really blistered both of them and told them next time she'd let them face the consequences if they did something stupid. Gordon said she chewed on them both so hard, she scared Herbert Faulkner forever. Gordon doesn't admit it, but I think she's always intimidated *him,* too."

Distracted, Buddy asked, "What had they done?"

"Hid a dead chicken in the vent pipes off the kitchen. Addie said it stunk even worse than skunk, and it took them a couple of days to find it."

"Why would they have done that?"

Max shrugged. "Who knows? Some people just like to make trouble."

"Do you know Uncle Gordon?"

"He's my uncle—step-uncle, anyway—so, sure.

He doesn't come very often, but when he does, he brings presents. Addie says it's to buy his way out of disfavor, but she takes what he brings."

"What does he bring?" Buddy was completely interested now.

"Oh, all kinds of stuff. A basket of fruit. A bag of shelled nuts. A box of high-priced candy. He brought me a neat knife." He fished it out of his pocket and opened it, displaying all the blades and the can opener and corkscrew and nail file, and a screwdriver. "Last time he brought Addie the complete Oxford English Dictionary she'd been wanting, so she doesn't have to go to the library every time she wants to look something up. Of course it's the whole twenty volumes packed into two big books, not the original full-sized set. Addie complains about having to use a magnifying glass to read it, but I can tell she really likes it. Even though she works at the library two days a week, she wanted the books handy here at home."

Buddy frowned, trying to remember what she knew about the Oxford English Dictionary. "It's not a regular dictionary, is it? Doesn't it tell when words were first used? Like back in 1610 or something?"

"Yeah. Lots of weird old words."

"Why does she want to look up weird old words?"

"She uses them in those stories she writes,"

Max said, coming down the steps with his hands in his pockets.

Buddy was astonished. "Addie writes stories?"

"Yeah. Never sells any of them, except once in a while a little short piece of some kind, to a magazine. The stories are historical novels. My old man says it's a waste of time. Nobody ever heard of her, and nobody'll ever buy anything from her. Didn't you notice the big envelope that came at lunchtime? She keeps sending them out, and everybody keeps sending them back with rejection slips. You watch, tomorrow she'll send that one out again to somebody new."

"I noticed it was addressed to Adelaide Ostrom, and they called her that at the school, too. But that's her maiden name, isn't it? Didn't she change her name when she got married?"

"Yeah. But she'd started writing under *Ostrom,* and she's kept on with that. Besides, she's lived in this town all her life, and everybody has known her as Addie Ostrom. Even when Ed was still alive, I think they called her Ostrom. Sometimes they call Cassie *Ostrom,* too, even though she's legally Mrs. Gus Miller."

Buddy was still intrigued by the idea that Addie wrote stories. "Are her stories any good?"

"I don't know. She never lets anybody read them. Probably not, or somebody would buy one, wouldn't they?"

"It seems sad, that she keeps getting rejections."

"Well, if she cries about it, she does it in private," Max stated.

The idea of Addie crying struck Buddy as being very strange indeed. Especially when she remembered how her aunt had spoken to the school principal. Addie was tough.

From behind them, through the open window into Grandpa's room, came the artificial-sounding voice of his speaking watch. "The time is 4:20 P.M."

Max rolled his eyes. "Now you understand why they made him move downstairs. It wasn't because he fell down the stairs, even if he did. It was because Addie couldn't stand the sound of that stupid watch going off every few minutes, even in the middle of the night. He pushes it every time he can't remember what time it is, which is all the time."

"And he can't see the clocks," Buddy mused. "It must be very hard to be almost blind."

"Yeah. It's hard on the rest of the family, too." Max kicked at a rock that bordered the pathway to the garden. "He's really upset because he can't see to read anymore. And even when somebody else reads to him, or he plays those tapes from the Services for the Blind, he can't remember until the next day what he's heard. You could read him the same thing, over and over, every day, and he wouldn't get tired of it, because he's already for-gotten it."

"Is that what you meant about the family being *dys—dysfunctional?* But he can't help it, can he?"

"No, he's not the one who's weird, except for being forgetful. It's the rest of them. Addie and Cassie and my old man. Hey, you smell that?"

"The roast?" Buddy asked, confused. Why would anyone look alarmed at the smell of cook-ing meat?

"No, not roast, it's paper. I hope he didn't start another fire—"

Max spun around and raced into the house, with Buddy at his heels. She could smell it, too, now: burning paper.

The kitchen was full of smoke. As they came in from the back hall, Cassie hurried into the room from the other direction. "Oh, Grandpa, what have you done?"

Max moved quickly toward the electric stove to turn off the burner that was glowing bright red. Then he reached for a metal spatula and shoved the burning newspaper off the burner into a dust-pan he'd grabbed out of a broom closet.

"He laid the paper on the stove again," he said.

"Grandpa, you mustn't turn on the stove," Cassie scolded him mildly, nudging him toward a chair at the table. "Don't you remember?"

"Time for tea," Grandpa said. "Isn't it?" He punched his watch and listened to it tell the time. "I was going to heat the water."

"But there's no teakettle," Cassie protested. She began to fan the smoke toward the back door, where Max had carried the still smoldering newspaper.

"I told you," Addie said, entering from the dining room. "We're going to have to take the knobs off that stove or he's going to burn the place down. In fact, I'm going to remove them right now. That's the second time in two weeks he's set something on fire."

"Aren't I going to get my tea, Sister?" Grandpa asked. "And maybe a cookie?"

"Well, I'll heat some water first. We could all use a cup of tea," Cassie said, opening a cupboard for cups. "It'll be awfully inconvenient to have to go hunting for the knobs when I need to use that stove, Addie."

"We'll keep them somewhere handy, where he won't find them. Better that than burning the house down around our ears. You're the one who thinks we should keep him at home, not put him in a rest home, where he belongs."

"Oh, Addie! You can't mean that! He's lived in this house since the day he was born! He'd be so upset if he had to move into a home. Everything would be so strange."

"You ask me," Max said, coming back with the empty dustpan, "things are strange enough around *here*."

Grandpa punched his watch button again, reactivating the tinny voice. "I wish you'd all talk louder. I can't make out a word you're saying."

Buddy had a peculiar feeling, one that must be somewhat like Alice's when she fell down the rabbit hole. Or was it at the Mad Hatter's Tea Party, where everybody said confusing things?

Cassie was putting tea bags into each of the cups. "Sit still, Grandpa. It'll be ready in a minute. And speaking of being ready, Buddy, it would be a good idea to get out your best go-to-meeting dress and make sure it doesn't need ironing. Better to do it now, if it needs it, than maybe forget until Sunday morning."

Buddy twitched. "Sunday morning? I didn't bring any dresses, Aunt Cassie. Just jeans and sweatshirts. I don't need to go to church—"

"Of course you'll go to church, with the rest of us. We *always* go to church as a family. The whole town would be shocked if we didn't take you. Everybody knows you're here."

"But Mama never sent me in jeans," Buddy protested.

"No, no, of course not. Addie, don't you think there's something among EllaBelle's old things that might fit her? A Sunday dress?"

"More than likely," Addie said. "Let's all have a cup of tea, and then we'll go look."

Somewhere in the bowels of the house, a telephone rang.

"Max, would you get that," Addie said, telling, not asking. "Your legs—"

"Are younger than yours," Max finished. He was back in a moment, just as Grandpa was checking once more on the time. "It's for her," he said, pointing at Buddy.

# 5

Buddy's fingers cramped around the receiver. "Hello?" she said breathlessly. "Bart?"

Her brother's voice sang along the line. "Yeah, it's me. You okay?"

"Yes. Did you find Dad?"

"Not yet. Listen, Rich Painter's missing, too. They were driving together. Neither he nor Dad checked in when they were supposed to the last time. I talked to Rich's mother, and she remembered the name of the trucking company in Lewiston that was hiring them. They took a load out from there to Sacramento, in California, and Rich called home from there when they delivered it. She thinks Dad tried to call us at the same time but didn't get anybody. It must have been that first week, when we went over to Devon's for the

55

barbecue party, remember? That's about the only time I can think of when we were both gone. Except, of course, when we were in school. I wish we'd had an answering machine, so we'd know for sure, but they were both okay when they left Sacramento."

Buddy felt as if a tight band around her chest had nearly cut off her breathing. "But what happened to them after that?"

"I'm still trying to find that out," Bart said. "I talked to the dispatcher at Edmonds Trucking in Lewiston, and he said they'd gone from Sacramento to Eureka, and they got there okay, too. I don't know why they didn't call us or Rich's mom from there—maybe they were loaded and left so early in the morning, they figured they didn't want to wake anybody up, so they intended to check in at home later. They were taking a load of lumber to L.A. Only they never got there."

"But that must have been days ago!" Buddy exclaimed. "How long could it have taken to drive from one end of California to the other?"

She heard her brother's indrawn breath. "Not this long, Buddy." Bart cleared his throat. "There seems to be some suspicion that . . . that Dad and Rich hijacked the load, maybe sold it to somebody. It was worth a lot of money."

Buddy's indignation exploded. "Dad never would have done anything like that!"

"You know it, I know it. But all the trucking company knows is that a couple of newly hired drivers disappeared with one of their trucks and a load of really expensive lumber."

"But that's crazy! How could they? You can't hide something as big as an eighteen-wheeler!"

"Not without really working at it. Edmonds has reported them to the police as missing. The California Highway Patrol is looking for them. But I'm afraid what they all think is that Dad and Rich deliberately disappeared after peddling their load for cash. They said there are lots of desolate places in northern California where they could have hidden a truck, or run it off a cliff where it wouldn't have been found right away."

There were unpleasant prickles along Buddy's spine. "No way," she said angrily, but there was more fear running through her than anger. "They don't know Dad!"

"No, but we do. I'm not giving up, Buddy. I'm going down to Eureka to see if I can pick up their trail. There are a lot of truckers running between there and San Francisco and Los Angeles, the whole length of California. Everybody runs with their CBs on; they must have talked to someone. It was a bright green truck with Edmonds' logo on the doors. Somebody must have seen it. They had to stop to eat and refuel. It may take me a few days, because I'll have to stop everywhere they might have stopped, talk to everybody who could have seen them or talked with them. So don't worry if you don't hear from me for a few days. I don't know how long it'll take. California's eight hundred miles long."

Buddy's throat was aching so, it was hard to speak. "Are you okay?"

"Sure. I keep the doors locked when I sleep in a rest stop or whatever. It'll be nice to sleep in a bed again, but it's not bad in the car. I don't want to waste cash on motels or anything like that. Aunt Cassie taking care of you all right?"

"I only got here this morning," Buddy reminded him. "She's a good cook, and they're nice." She didn't mention what Max had said about her relatives being a dysfunctional family. "Aunt Addie signed me up to go to school if you don't get back before Monday."

"Not much chance of that, Buddy. Just go, do the best you can. I'll call you when I find Dad, even if I can't get up there to get you right away."

"It won't be very long, will it?" There was a tremor in her voice.

"I don't know. I hope not. Take care, Buddy. Don't give up hope. I'll find him and Rich, or maybe the police will find them first. But they're figuring stuff like hijacking a load, and I'm not, so we're looking in different places, I guess. Even if I don't find Dad right away, I'll come get you. Okay?"

She was so choked, she could barely echo his okay. If he didn't find Dad, what would happen to them both? Bart wasn't even out of high school yet, and he had no skills to enable him to support them both.

She hung up, fighting tears.

She didn't want to walk back into the kitchen and see those questioning faces, but there was no choice. They were still drinking their tea, except for Max, who was swigging a can of pop.

"Any news of Dan?" Cassie asked.

She shook her head. "Bart's going to Eureka, the last place he took a load."

Max studied her face, then offered, "You want a Coke?"

Her throat hurt, and she wasn't sure she could swallow, but maybe trying would be better than what she was feeling right now. Only when she tried to speak, her voice didn't work. Max went to the refrigerator, got another can, and popped the top for her.

It stung when she sipped at it, but that was a distraction from the pain that enveloped her. She didn't think she could bear it if Bart didn't find Dad so that everything would be all right.

"Well," Addie said, standing up, and carrying her cup to the dishwasher, "let's go see what we can find for you to wear to church, girl."

She'd never in her life felt less like going to

church, but she didn't know any way to get out of it. She followed Addie through the house and up the stairs. They went past the open door to Addie's room, and two closed doors on the other side of the hall, into the room Buddy might have had if it hadn't been full of junk.

There were lots of cardboard cartons, all of them neatly labeled, stacked nearly to the ceiling in half of the room. There was also, surprisingly, a desk and a computer and printer in the other half.

And there was Addie's Oxford English Dictionary, along with a few other books beside the monitor.

Addie wasn't looking at the materials for her writing, however. She was moving cartons, searching for a particular one. "Here, these are some of EllaBelle's things. No, this batch is stuff she left when she ran away, and never sent for. There should be another one of older stuff, when she was younger."

"She ran away?" Buddy echoed, forgetting to drink her soda. "Mama ran away?"

"Eloped." Addie sent her a glance, then returned to her search. "Didn't she ever tell you that? Never warned a soul. Just packed a suitcase and left a note. 'Dan and I are getting married. Will write.' Had the entire town in shock."

People *did* elope all the time, didn't they? Why should that have sent the entire town into shock?

After all, who did it matter to, except maybe her family, who hadn't been expecting it.

"Ah, this should be the one," Addie said, carrying a box over to set it on the bed. "Let's see what we've got."

The dresses she began to unpack caught Buddy's interest even though she wasn't much interested in clothes, especially right now. She could imagine her mother wearing that pale lavender one with the lacy collar, and the blue and white check, and the navy blue with the sailor collar. "These are beautiful," Buddy murmured, putting down her Coke can on the edge of the desk.

"I made them all for her," Addie said. "We all pampered her. And even so, she did what she did."

"'What she did'?" Buddy asked, but Addie wasn't paying any attention.

"Ah, maybe this one. It looked wonderful on her. I made it for her fifteenth birthday celebration. A grown-up dress, she wanted. Let's see if taking it in a little will make it fit. Take off your clothes."

Feeling numb, Buddy obeyed. The dress was apricot-colored, very simple, and only a little bit loose on her. She didn't resist when Addie twirled her around, inspecting her.

"I didn't think it would be out of style. Classic designs never are. If I take it in a smidgen, it should be about right. Let me get a few pins."

Buddy's mind felt jumbled. Her mother had run away, and shocked the whole town, and done something that was not good. Something that made the family angry with her.

There were so many questions she wanted to ask, but she didn't quite dare. What had her mother done to Addie that had estranged them enough so that Addie didn't write to her younger sister? Even Cassie, seemingly so much easier going, hadn't written very often. Mama had missed the letters, Buddy knew, though she hadn't talked about it except for once when Buddy had overheard her parents talking about it.

"It hurts when they don't answer me, Dan," EllaBelle had said. "We used to be so close. I suppose Cassie's just too busy now, running the house and taking care of Grandpa since our mom and dad died." And Dad had hugged her and they had stopped talking when they had realized Buddy was listening.

"Turn around," Addie said now, and obediently Buddy stood and held her arms out of the way of the sticking pins. "Your mother looked like an angel in this. It was her first boy-girl party, and she was beautiful. Okay, take it off—be careful of the pins—and I'll take a couple of the seams in."

Buddy felt confused and uncertain. One minute Addie talked about how beautiful EllaBelle had been, and the next she made remarks suggesting that her younger sister had done something that had alienated them, but with no explanation that Buddy could understand.

The sewing machine in the corner was quite a contrast to the computer-printer setup. It was an old treadle machine, which Addie used expertly; then she pressed the new seams into place before Buddy tried the dress on again. Another of the oddly assorted items in this back bedroom was a full-length mirror, and Buddy was astonished at her own appearance.

"Now all we need is to do something with your hair," Addie said critically.

Buddy stared at the offending dark mass. "It won't curl," she said. "We've tried."

"A new cut, then," Addie decided. "It's too long to style if it won't curl. Mine never would, either. That's why I keep it short. Cassie's a whiz with the scissors."

Alarmed, Buddy touched the ends that hung down over the apricot dress. "I'm used to it this way."

Addie had a way of not noticing statements that didn't jibe with her own perception of things. "Shoes. Good grief, you can't wear athletic shoes with that dress."

Buddy looked down at them. "They're the only ones I have with me."

"What size do you wear? Maybe a pair of mine

would work. Sandals. Yes, let me check on sandals."

They found a pair in Addie's closet, close enough to a fit so Buddy thought she could wear them long enough to attend church. Back at the mirror, she had to admit they looked much nicer than her own shoes.

"Okay. Let's go consult Cassie about your hair," Addie said, as if Cassie's opinion, and her own, were the only ones that mattered.

Cassie didn't ask Buddy for her opinion, either. Though Buddy made a little squawking protest, they sat her down on a kitchen chair and whipped out an enveloping cape to keep the hair off her new dress, and Cassie got out the scissors.

"I've been cutting hair since I was not much older than you are," Cassie assured her as she began to snip.

Long strands of dark brown hair fell onto the cape, and Buddy watched in dismay as more and more of it fell around her. It was all she could do not to cry. She'd never been especially vain about her hair—after all, it was straight and ordinary—but it was *her* hair. Would it be this way with everything if she had to stay here for long? With someone else making all the decisions that should be her own? It made her feel as if the person she really was was insignificant, that only with improvements could she be found acceptable.

"There!" Cassie said finally. "What do you think, Addie?"

Addie grunted. "Just like one of those models we saw on TV. Getting rid of the hair makes your eyes look bigger. She's the spitting image of Ella-Belle, isn't she?"

Cassie stood back to inspect her own work. "Go take a look, Buddy. There's another tall mirror in the front hallway. Turn on the light so you can really see."

Dreading the stranger who was going to appear before her, Buddy trudged through the dining room to the hall and flicked the light switch.

And stranger she was. But the dark hair, always so unruly and without form, now lay about her head in a perfect, close-fitting cap, with the slightest of waves at her temples and just below her ears. Addie had followed her and made a sound of satisfaction. "It was too heavy before. Pulled out what little wave you had. This is perfect."

The girl in the mirror certainly didn't look like Buddy Adams. Buddy's resistance melted away. She looked almost pretty.

They heard a door open in the rear of the house, and a man's voice called out, "Where is everybody? How long till supper?"

"Oh, Gus is home," Addie said flatly. "Take the dress off before you mess it up. You'll need nylons, too. Mine would be too long for you and Cassie's too wide. I'll pick up a pair tomorrow on my way to work."

"Work?" Buddy echoed, distracted from her own suddenly intriguing image.

"Work. I run the library, such as it is. Open every Thursday and Saturday. You'll take Haysville by storm," she predicted, then added drily, "just like your mother did. She always was the family beauty."

After she'd turned away, Buddy lingered for a moment, turning this way and that, as a growing delight filled her. She looked older than eleven, and quite smart with the new dress and the awesome hairstyle.

Even after she'd changed back into jeans and a sweatshirt, the haircut remained. Simple, yet elegant. That had been one of Mama's phrases. She'd liked things that were simple, yet elegant. Until now, Buddy had never imagined that those words could pertain to herself.

She didn't know what Dad and Bart would think, but she decided that *she* was pleased, after all.

Uncle Gus was at the refrigerator with the door open, selecting a bottle of beer. He turned and stared at her. "Well, who's this?"

"You remember, I told you Buddy was coming for a few days," Cassie said. She was stirring something on the stove while Addie set the table. "Buddy, this is Uncle Gus."

He was a stocky, middle-aged man, going bald on top but overdue for a haircut. He needed suspenders to hold his pants up over a large belly, red ones over a black and yellow plaid shirt. "Buddy? Funny name for a girl," he observed, hooking a chair with a booted foot and pulling it out to sink down at the table with his beer.

"It's a nickname," Buddy said stiffly. "My real name is Amy Kate."

"Now who'd give a pretty little girl a name like Buddy?" he asked, flipping the cap of his bottle toward the nearest wastebasket, and missing. He took a long drink and stared at her some more.

"My dad started calling me that when I was little," Buddy said. "I used to go everywhere with him, even on the truck when he was driving, and he called me his little Buddy."

Gus apparently lost interest in her at that point and turned his attention to his son. Max was perched on a stool near the counter, putting slices of cucumber and tomato on beds of lettuce in a series of salad plates set out in front of him.

"I heard you kids got in trouble in school again, shut down a couple of classrooms."

Max gave him a look that appeared to denote distaste. "Not me," he denied. "Some of the other kids. Only closed one classroom and the library."

"You want to watch it," Gus said, anyway. "I know you kids all think old Faulkner is a joke of a principal, but he can kick you out of school. I'll tell you, you get expelled, no way I'm driving you over to Kalispell to school."

Max's jaws clenched visibly. "I'm not getting kicked out of school, Pa."

"When I was a kid, I got in trouble in school. I was in more trouble when I got home. My old man lit into me with his belt."

Buddy was watching Max and saw the expression that came over his face. Max was smaller than his father, but Buddy was suddenly convinced that he would resist to his utmost if Gus tried to whip him.

*A dysfunctional family,* Max had said. She hadn't asked Bart for a definition, but she had a pretty good idea what Max had been talking about. She didn't think she cared for Uncle Gus very much.

"How come nobody ever feeds me?" Grandpa asked from the doorway of his room. He pushed the button to activate the voice on his watch. "Is supper all over?"

"No, Grandpa, it's not ready yet," Cassie said.

The old man wandered across the room toward the area where food was being prepared. "I smell cucumbers. Don't put any in my salad, Sister."

"Max is making them separate, and no cucumbers in yours. Go sit down, honey. It'll be ready in a few minutes."

Grandpa tapped out with his cane and located a chair. "Did you know Blackie came back? He was lost, but he came back."

"No, Grandpa, Blackie didn't come back," Addie said, steering him into the chair. "Blackie died, remember?"

"No, he didn't. He's sleeping on my bed right now. Been there all afternoon."

"My kitten!" Max said, suddenly agitated. "That's where he went!"

He left his salad assembly line and trotted over to the open door to the old man's room. "Hey, there you are, you scamp. That's what I'm going to call him, Scamp."

Gus was scowling. "Where'd you get that critter? You know I don't like cats."

"I'll keep him out of your way," Max said, cradling the kitten.

"I like cats," Grandpa said. "I always had cats around the house, and the store, too." He hesitated, an odd, rather lost expression coming over his face. "Do I still have the store?"

"No, Grandpa. You sold the store after you had a stroke," Addie told him.

Grandpa's forehead wrinkled up as he tried to remember. "I sold the store?"

"Yes. To Alf Peterson."

The forehead got more wrinkled. "I never liked Alf Peterson."

"Neither did anyone else, but he paid you in cash. And you couldn't keep running the place anymore."

"Cash," Grandpa repeated. "There *was* a lot of cash, wasn't there? A big pile. A whole bag full."

Suddenly the room was full of tension.

Buddy didn't have the slightest idea why, but she stiffened, feeling as if the air had abruptly turned blue.

Cassie forgot to stir the gravy she was making. Addie paused with the last napkin in her hand, not placing it on the table. Gus rested his beer bottle on the table and seemed almost to be holding his breath.

And Max . . . when Buddy's gaze swept toward him, Max was staring at *her.*

Whatever the problem, Buddy thought, Max knew what it was. And somehow it involved her, though she couldn't imagine how that could be.

And then, as if someone had hit the *pause* button on a remote control, freezing all the action, it was as if the *play* button had been activated, and motion resumed.

# 6

The atmosphere at the supper table was quite different from what it had been at lunch, and Buddy knew exactly why.

Gus dominated what conversation there was. Max said nothing at all unless someone directly addressed him. He had put down another bowl for the kitten and was watching him, avoiding his father's attention as much as he could.

Gus talked about the fellows down at the Hayloft, the local tavern. He talked about sporting events and scores. He informed them that there was a Seahawks-Raiders game on the satellite at seven o'clock, if they wanted to watch.

Nobody rose to the bait. Bart and Dad had watched football games on TV, especially when the Seattle team was playing, and often Buddy had joined them to cheer on the Seahawks. It had always been a fun evening, and they'd popped corn or baked pizza and sipped soft drinks.

Gus slurped beer.

The cooking was excellent. Buddy realized how poorly she and her own family had been fed since Mom was gone, depending on simple recipes with little seasoning, or take-out foods, or frozen dinners. They hadn't tasted anything like this beef roasted with potatoes and carrots and onions. Their salads hadn't been topped by sunflower seeds and slices of pale green avocado.

Yet nobody complimented the cook. Gus rose in the middle of the meal and got another bottle of beer. "Listen," he said to Max. "You get that front yard mowed tomorrow, you hear?"

Max nodded, not speaking.

"And you'd better bundle up them old newspapers and get 'em over to the recycling bin."

Cassie cleared her throat. "I was hoping you might have time to put up the storm windows tomorrow, Gus. We haven't had any bad weather yet this year, but last year this time we got that big blow, and the first snow."

Gus gave her a disgusted look. "And I hurt my back getting them windows in, don't you remember? Listen, if Max can't manage 'em, why don't you go ahead and hire somebody to do it? Jim Silva's always looking for a small job to pick up a little extra."

Addie spoke for the first time since Grandpa had been asked to say grace, which he did surprisingly well. "And where did you figure we were going to get the money to pay Jim?"

"Didn't you just get a check from Gordon? I saw the envelope on the dining room table. Good old rich Gordon, he always comes through, don't he?"

Addie's lips thinned. "The money Gordon sent was to buy new tires for the car, so we'll feel safe enough to drive into Kalispell if we have to. We can't ask Gordon to pay for everything. It's a good thing Daddy left us a little annuity to keep this place running, but he never figured on what inflation was going to be like, and there isn't enough to go around for anything luxurious."

"Didn't bother you to ask him to buy you that computer, did it? That must have set him back a bundle."

"He lent me the money for the computer. I'll pay him back when I sell something," Addie defended herself. "And it's none of your business, anyway, Gus."

"Yeah, well, I hope he ain't holding his breath, waiting for you to sell one of them romancy novels of yours. At least Gordon's making enough money so he can afford to waste some of it. I'm sure not. My disability pension ain't enough to cover much but the essentials," Gus said, helping himself to two more biscuits and slathering them with butter.

Suddenly he jumped sideways and glared at Grandpa. "For crying out loud, look what you did! You got it all over me!"

Cassie was on her feet, hustling for a dish towel to wipe up the spilled water. "You know he can't see a glass of water. It's the same as invisible."

"Then let him sit next to somebody else," Gus grumbled, wiping at his pants.

Grandpa activated his watch. "Is it time for *Jeopardy!?*" he wanted to know.

"Not for half an hour yet," Cassie told him. "Finish your supper, honey."

They all finished in silence. Buddy was glad nobody expected her to speak up while Gus was there.

He was the first to push back his chair. "Got to get moving," he said, as if he had an appointment. "That bowling match starts in just a bit. Got me a little bet on that Scheffler fella, bet he's going to come out on top."

Again, Addie's mouth pinched up. Gus couldn't afford to help pay someone to put up the storm windows, but he could put a bet on a bowling game, and he could sit at the tavern all evening, no doubt buying more beers. Buddy was beginning to understand why Addie wondered how Cassie could have married the man.

She realized that Max was looking at her. When he saw that she'd noticed, he shrugged. "You look different with your hair cut that way."

She'd almost forgotten that. She couldn't tell from his tone whether he thought she looked better or worse.

Gus was nearly out of the kitchen when he stepped in the kitten's bowl, and maybe on his tail, too, because he yowled and leaped away from him. Gus swore. "There's no way you're keeping that critter where people can trip over him," he said to Max, who was already on his feet to rescue the newly named Scamp.

"I want Blackie to sit in my lap while I listen to *Jeopardy!,* like he used to do," Grandpa said, getting up, too.

"He's not Blackie, Grandpa, he's my new kitten," Max protested, but Grandpa was already reaching for the small animal.

Instinctively, Max clutched the kitten tighter, looking beseechingly at Cassie. "He's mine, not Grandpa's Blackie."

"Oh, Max, let him take the cat," Cassie urged. "Of course he's yours, and he'll probably forget all about it by tomorrow. Let Grandpa hold him for a while now. Buddy, you want to help me clear the table?"

Buddy saw Max's expression and wished she could help. His jaw was clenched as he handed over the kitten and let the old man carry him toward the living room.

Nobody else was interested in listening to *Jeopardy!* The atmosphere changed when Gus had gone, though. Buddy could feel everybody relaxing. Cassie got out a basket of mending, Addie announced that she was going up to work on the computer, and Max muttered something about running next door to Jeremy's house for a few minutes.

That left Buddy with little to do.

In the living room, which was large and comfortable, with two couches and several recliner chairs—all but one of them old and shabby—she found a tall bookshelf. Grandpa was settled in front of the TV with the remote in his hand, with his program on loud enough to make her ears hurt.

The books were mostly ones she remembered her mother talking about from many years ago, most of which Buddy had read, too. But there, on one middle shelf, were some with newer covers and titles. Nothing for kids, but then she often read books that Bart or Dad brought home.

She took two of the most likely looking ones and decided to carry them back to the sewing room that was now her own. She could still hear the television, but at least it didn't make her ears ache.

She didn't really feel like reading, though. She couldn't stop thinking about her brother, out there somewhere sleeping in rest stops, asking people if they'd seen an eighteen-wheeler, the sleeper cab painted bright green with an EDMONDS TRUCKING logo on the door. He'd be asking if they remembered Dad or Rich, and describing them. She prayed somebody would know what had happened to keep them from delivering their load as scheduled. She prayed Dad was safe, and that Bart would be, too.

Halfheartedly, Buddy opened one of the books and began to read. It was a true story of someone whose yard and home had been invaded by a bear cub, and it was both touching and funny, entertaining enough so that she gradually got engrossed in the antics of the bear.

She hadn't closed the door into the little room, so she looked up at once when Cassie tapped on the doorframe.

"We're all going to have a snack before bedtime," Cassie said. "You want to come out and join us?"

Buddy was surprised to realize she'd been reading for several hours. She put the book aside and followed her aunt toward the kitchen. She could hear Grandpa there, checking the time, and met Addie coming down the stairs at the same time as Max came in the back door.

Everybody was there except Gus.

"I'm heating some milk for cocoa," Cassie said to all of them as they assembled in the kitchen. "There are some chocolate cookies to go with it. Shall we sit around the table here?"

The kitten had gotten off Grandpa's lap when he'd left the TV behind, and Max was quick to snatch him up and cradle him against his chest.

"How come I don't have the store anymore?" Grandpa asked plaintively, sitting down in one of the old oak chairs.

"You sold it, honey," Cassie said, checking the pan of milk on the stove.

"I didn't want to sell it," Grandpa said. "I worked in that store my whole adult life. Didn't I?"

"You sure did," Cassie agreed.

"I always gave people a good deal. Fair prices. Good service. Everybody in town came in there to buy their furniture and appliances."

"That's right," Cassie confirmed.

"Then why did I sell it?"

Cassie and Addie exchanged a look, and once more Buddy sensed mysterious currents that she couldn't interpret. "You had a stroke, Grandpa," Addie told him, bringing out the plate of cookies. "You couldn't work anymore."

"How long ago was that?"

"About two and a half years ago. Here, you want one of these?"

"I always want a cookie." Grandpa reached to take one and noticed Buddy, just sitting down across from him. "Who's this?"

"You remember. Buddy," Cassie said. "Ella-Belle's girl."

He nodded. "Where's EllaBelle?"

This time the current swirled for only seconds before Addie said calmly, "She died, Grandpa. In a car wreck."

"She did? Was he driving? That fellow she married?"

"No, she was alone when it happened. She skidded on the ice."

Grandpa nibbled thoughtfully. "Always liked that boy. Dan, wasn't that his name?"

"Yes." Again, Addie was tight-lipped. Why? Buddy wondered. Why did she get that way at the mention of her father?

"Dan. I remember," Grandpa said. He had carried the remote control with him and placed it on the table. "He worked for me in the store, didn't he? Best salesman I ever had. Except for myself. He was almost as good as I was."

That was true enough. If he'd wanted a sales job, he could have found one that didn't take him on the road, Buddy thought, and the prickle of tears made her blink. But in spite of his ability to sell anything to anybody, he'd didn't really like that line of work. Buddy remembered exactly what he'd said. "I hate selling people things they don't need and can't afford. I'd rather have a straightforward job like working in the mill or driving a truck, where I'm not taking advantage of anybody."

She wished with all her heart that he'd wanted to take a nice, safe job in a store or a lumberyard.

"Is he here?" Grandpa asked. "Dan? Won't he come and say hello?"

"No. He's . . . not here," Addie told him. "Who on earth is that at this time of night?" The doorbell had rung, echoing through the house. "I'll go see."

It couldn't be Bart, or Dad, but Buddy's heart leaped, anyway. Maybe there was word of them. . . . She waited, holding her breath, hearing Addie's voice, and a male voice answering, from off in the distance.

Buddy couldn't understand anything that was being said at the front door, but Max must have caught some of it, because he suddenly started to move in that direction. "Something's happened to Pa," he said.

Cassie turned off the burner under the milk. "Gus?" she said, and quickly followed Max.

Grandpa seemed not to have understood anything that had been said. Maybe he hadn't even heard any of it. He looked toward Buddy—seeing only a black spot where her face would be, she remembered—and asked, "Where's my cocoa? Didn't somebody say we were having cocoa?"

Curious, yet unwilling to join the others, Buddy offered, "I'll pour the milk for you. I think the cocoa's already in the cups."

She mixed only Grandpa's, however, and carried it to the table. "It's hot," she warned.

"Only way to drink cocoa is hot," the old man told her. "I remember your mama and daddy, Sister. They ran away and got married. I thought it was just what they ought to have done, but some people didn't like it." He screwed up his face, trying to force a recollection that wouldn't come. "I don't remember why they were so upset, though. Do you know?"

"No, I don't," Buddy said, her mouth going dry.

Grandpa sighed. "I forget things. Some days I remember just fine, and then other times I can't recall a thing. Sister cried, I think. Late at night, when everybody else was asleep. I heard her crying. My room was right across from hers. And there was another time when Sister cried. I can't remember why, that time. Now they make me sleep downstairs. So I won't fall, Sister says. I only fell the one time. Broke my arm. Couldn't arm wrestle. Can you arm wrestle?"

"Not very well," Buddy said. "My brother always beats me."

"Let's see," the old man proposed, and reached out across the table toward her.

The movement was unexpected, and he couldn't see what was directly in front of him. The cup overturned, and the brown cocoa splashed out across the table, onto the plate of cookies and the remote control beside it.

"Oh, oh. Sister's going to be annoyed with me again. I spilled something, didn't I?"

Buddy was on her feet, going for a dish towel, mopping up the mess. Some of the cookies were beyond help, but she rescued the ones she could.

Suddenly she could hear the voices from the front of the house more clearly. "Maybe we ought to take him to the hospital," Cassie was saying anxiously. "That's a nasty-looking cut. It needs stitches."

"I think we can butterfly it together," Addie said. "Run and get the tape and some gauze, Max. Can you walk, Gus, as far as the kitchen, where there's a better light? Cassie, a basin and a washcloth. The tape won't stick until we get the bleeding stopped and dry up the blood beside the cut."

"But what if he has a concussion?" Cassie persisted.

"Cassie, our car is in no shape to drive him to the hospital. Not with those tires. I haven't had a chance to get the new ones yet. Come on, Gus, make an effort to help us, will you? Walk right over there and sit down."

Buddy, still with the cocoa-soaked towel in her hands, leaped out of the way, shocked at the bloody spectacle.

"Head cuts always bleed profusely," Addie said. She spared a glance for Buddy's reaction. "He isn't going to die of it." Her tone suggested that this might be a pity.

Gus sagged into the chair and slumped forward on his elbows, but Addie jerked him upright.

"I can't do this unless you cooperate. Tilt your head backward and hold it that way."

"Sick to my stomach," Gus muttered.

"Well, don't throw up until Cassie gets a basin. Hurry, Cass, it's coming up!"

Buddy turned away, not wanting to watch. It was bad enough to listen to the man retching. She took the towel to the sink and dropped it there.

In the middle of all the confusion, Grandpa checked the time. "10:06 P.M.," said the tinny voice.

Max returned with his supplies. "There's not much tape, except the little strips."

"Those'll do. Here, now that his stomach's empty, hold his head up for me. He's too drunk to do it on his own. Gus, make an effort, will you?"

Buddy thought the most helpful thing she could do might be to get Grandpa out of the area. "I'll give you another cup of cocoa and you can drink it in your room, all right, Grandpa?" she asked.

"Is it still hot?" the old man asked, but he didn't resist when she steered him toward his bedroom.

It was more crowded than either the back bedroom upstairs or the sewing room. Buddy settled him into a platform rocker and placed the steaming cup in his hands after looking in vain for a place to set it down.

Beside his bed, there were tables and chests

and shelves full of books he surely could not read any longer, and boxes and bundles of all kinds. There was hardly room to walk between them and the bed.

"This is not my room," Grandpa said.

Buddy didn't know what to say to that.

"My room was always upstairs," the old man told her. "Why did they make me move down here, Sister?"

"I don't know," Buddy said.

"I remember you," he told her. "I just can't remember your name."

"They call me Buddy, but my real name's Amy Kate."

"Amy Kate. That's a pretty name. When you were a little girl you used to come to the store and eat my butterscotch drops, didn't you?"

"Yes," Buddy admitted, and then wondered if he was thinking of her or her mother. "My mom's name was EllaBelle."

"Oh, yes. EllaBelle. She ran away with Dan, and Sister cried. That's right."

Because there was no one else around to hear, and she guessed Grandpa wouldn't have any memory of this conversation, Buddy asked impulsively, "Which sister, Grandpa? Which one cried? And why?"

Grandpa sipped from his cocoa. "Just the way I liked it. Almost *too* hot. You always did make good cocoa, Sister."

Buddy sighed. It was no use. Sometimes he would be perfectly sensible for a few minutes, and then his mind seemed to drift away to something else—another subject, another time.

"Can I get you anything else before I go, Grandpa?" she asked.

"No, no. It's not time for me to go to bed, is it?"

"I don't know what time you go to bed," Buddy told him. "It's only a little after ten."

"I haven't seen the news, have I? The eleven o'clock news. Or does it come on at ten?"

"I don't know," she said again. "The Seattle stations mostly have news at eleven."

"I'll drink my cocoa first. While it's hot," he decided, and rocked a little in his chair.

Back in the kitchen, Buddy decided to reheat one cup of milk in the microwave and make herself a cup of cocoa. She didn't know if any of the others would come back and want some or not.

She heard Max on the stairs, and turned to see him scooping up the kitten that had been left behind when the others scattered. She was glad Grandpa had forgotten about him.

"Did Blackie die a long time ago?" she asked.

"Before I ever came here to live. Probably twenty years ago. Grandpa gets all mixed up about when it is." His mouth was tight and unpleasant, but he was stroking the kitten, so that Buddy could hear him purring.

Buddy stirred the cocoa mix into her cup.

"I'm . . . sorry about your dad. He's not badly hurt, is he? Or should they call a doctor?"

"No doctor in Haysville." Max sounded sullen, angry. And then he practically exploded, his face twisting as if in fury. "One of these days I hope he falls down drunk and breaks his neck!"

She didn't know if he meant it or not, and she didn't get a chance to ask. He hugged the kitten against his chest and went back upstairs, leaving Buddy alone.

She supposed it was late enough to go to bed. She got into her pajamas and crawled into the made-up bed in the sewing room. It was comfortable—certainly more so than the car had been for sleeping—but strange. It even smelled different. And it certainly wasn't home.

She didn't have a home anymore, Buddy reminded herself. Right this minute she didn't even have a family.

She'd forgotten to say her prayers, but she didn't want to get back up to kneel beside the bed, so she said them lying flat on her back, looking up into the darkness. *Please, let Bart find Dad. Let them both be all right.*

She didn't think she'd be able to sleep very soon, but she was just drifting off when she heard what sounded like something exploding, and then heard Cassie crying, "Oh, no, Grandpa! What did you do?"

"Good grief," Addie said, loudly enough to carry to the sewing room also. "This place is a madhouse!"

There was a small crash. Buddy slid out of bed and headed for the kitchen to find out what the latest catastrophe was. Her heart was pounding so hard that her chest hurt.

# 7

Grandpa stood staring at the microwave, wobbling a little as he leaned on his cane. Around his feet were the shards of his cup, with a small puddle of remaining cocoa running down his pant leg.

Buddy stumbled to a halt, balancing with one hand on the back of a chair. Max gingerly opened the microwave and said incredulously, "He put the remote control in here."

Addie, who had arrived simultaneously with Buddy, was equally disbelieving. "Judging by those black marks inside the oven, he's blown it up. Both the remote and the microwave. What on earth were you thinking, Grandpa?"

The old man looked as if he was about to cry. "I did something wrong, didn't I, Sister?"

Cassie was once more cleaning up a mess. She

must have been about out of dish towels by now, Buddy thought.

"What did you mean to do, Grandpa?" Cassie asked, looking up at him as she gathered up the broken china bits.

"It didn't work," he said in a faltering voice. "I tried to listen to the news, but it wouldn't work. I figured it was because it was wet, and I thought I could dry it out. . . ."

Across the room, Buddy sucked in a breath of guilty distress. Should she have taken the remote away from him after the cocoa was spilled on it? Told Addie or Cassie?

Max was examining the remains of the remote. "I think it melted all its innards."

"And ruined the microwave," Addie said grimly.

"I thought it would just dry it out. You know, heat it up until it got dry," Grandpa said.

Buddy had figured out by this time that there was not enough income to take care of emergencies like worn-out tires and replacing remote controls and microwaves. She cleared her throat, and they all looked at her.

"I guess . . . maybe I should have done something about it. When the remote got wet. I never thought about what he'd do with it. . . ."

"We lived before we had a microwave," Cassie said quietly. "Or a remote control. Come on, Grandpa, I think it's time you went to bed. You kids, too." She dropped the wet dish towel into the sink and left it there, too tired to rinse it out.

Grandpa didn't resist her urging until he reached his bedroom door. Then he paused and turned around. "Where's Blackie? Blackie always sleeps with me."

Buddy saw the dismay on Max's face as he made a small sound of protest.

Cassie opened her mouth and said, "Max—"

But Addie spoke firmly before her sister could finish the thought. "Blackie's dead, Grandpa. He got hit by a car, and he's gone."

"He's gone? Blackie's gone?"

"Years ago. Max has a new kitten, but he's not Blackie. Go on, now, go to bed. You, Buddy, get to bed, too. It wasn't your fault he can't think straight anymore. Max, keep the cat out of his sight if you can. He'll forget about him if he doesn't see him."

Max muttered, "Thanks, Addie," and headed toward the stairs before Cassie could countermand that order.

Buddy had reached the door of the sewing room before she realized that she was thirsty. She had nearly reached the kitchen again for a glass of water when she heard her aunts' voices.

"He won't forget Blackie," Cassie was saying. "He remembers things from a long time ago quite well. It's just what's happening now that he can't get a grasp on."

"So what are you saying? That we should make Max give up his kitten so Grandpa can pretend he's Blackie? That's hardly fair to Max, is it? Did you get Gus settled down in bed?"

"Yes, he went right to sleep. I still think maybe we ought to get him to the hospital so they can X-ray his head." Cassie twisted her hands together. "Just in case he *does* have a concussion or a fractured skull."

"I could feel the bone all around the cut. It's perfectly solid. So it's not fractured, but it might be concussed. If you want to take the car over to Kurt's in the morning and have him put the new tires on so it's feasible to take him into Kalispell, go ahead. I can't go with you, though. I have to open up the library."

"Maybe Max would like to go with me," Cassie suggested tentatively.

"And maybe he wouldn't," Addie said. "He's furious with Gus, you know. He *hates* the way Gus drinks and disgraces himself. Why should you punish Max by dragging him along? He's got a day planned already, remember? He has work to do here at home, and Gus is going to feel rotten tomorrow, so he'll be even nastier than usual, to whoever is present in the car. And I know Max is expecting to do something with his buddies during the afternoon. Give him a break, Cassie. And about the kitten, too. It is *his* kitten."

Buddy was holding her breath. She had stopped out of their sight because she didn't want to get into the middle of another one of their embarrassing conversations. If she hadn't been so thirsty, she'd have gone back to bed without a drink, but she couldn't get to the bathroom without being seen, either.

"But Grandpa thinks he's Blackie," Cassie was saying now. "He's going to be so upset. He thinks he has Blackie again."

"For pete's sake, Cassie, Grandpa is senile! He's not logical! He can't remember anything from one minute to the next! Does that mean we all have to give in to him every time he does or wants something unreasonable?"

"You just want to put him in a rest home and get rid of him," Cassie said, sounding as if she was going to cry.

Addie was explosive. "No, I don't! I'll admit that some things about him drive me crazy—like punching that clock every thirty seconds! But I've loved him as long as you have—longer, because I'm older—and I want him to be safe. I want *us* to be safe. Sticking that remote control in the microwave was not a rational thing to do, and we have to recognize that he can't help doing things that are irrational. In a rest home they'd be better equipped to watch him day and night, and he couldn't demand to have someone else's cat and claim it for his own. And maybe we could have a peaceful night's sleep without worrying that he'll burn the house down around our ears."

"I don't mind sleeping light, listening for him," Cassie said.

Buddy shifted her weight, not wanting to listen, yet not quite able to walk away, either. She hoped Cassie wouldn't think of asking *her* to ride along as company to take Gus to the hospital, because she was sure Addie was right about one thing: Gus would not be a pleasant companion with both a hangover and a head injury. She bit her lip and waited.

Addie sighed. "Do what you like about taking Gus to Kalispell. But let Max keep his kitten. Explain—a hundred times, if necessary—that this one belongs to Max. And Cassie, don't ask Buddy to go with you tomorrow, either."

Buddy's heart fluttered.

Although they were speaking in normal tones and she wasn't having any trouble catching every word, she strained to hear more clearly.

"You think I'm not fair," Cassie challenged her sister. "But you aren't, either, Addie."

Buddy wondered how much more exasperated Addie could get without the two of them coming to actual blows.

"What are you talking about now?"

"It's not fair to hold . . . the way you feel about

EllaBelle . . . against Buddy. She can't help what her mother did."

Buddy's throat closed, and she pressed a hand against it. *"What her mother did"? What did* that *mean?*

Addie gave a snort of anger. "I don't hold anything against Buddy. And just because she's the spitting image of EllaBelle at that age doesn't mean I don't know she's an entirely different person. Why on earth do you think I'm being unfair to her? I got out the clothes, with a painful memory in every stitch I had put into every dress, and altered one to fit the child, didn't I?"

Buddy wished she'd died of thirst and stayed in her little sewing room, yet she couldn't leave now. Why were there painful memories in the clothes Addie had made for her mother? That didn't make any sense at all.

"I can tell by the way you look at her," Cassie asserted quietly. "I see you studying her when she doesn't notice you're looking."

"Oh, for the love of—!" Addie smacked a hand on the back of a chair. "She does look exactly like her mother, and I'm reminded of difficult things when I look at Buddy, but I certainly don't dislike her or blame her for the money being gone. I'm going to bed. You're impossible to talk to tonight. You're even more irrational than Grandpa is," she said as she headed directly for where Buddy was standing.

In a panic, Buddy stumbled backward and pressed herself into the open doorway to the sewing room, nearly falling.

She didn't have time to close the door before Addie passed, but since there was no light in the room, she didn't notice Buddy.

Buddy's heart hammered at the close call, and with dismay at the things she'd heard. What had Addie meant about not blaming her for the money being gone? What money? It sounded as if Addie had *hated* her mother, yet if that was the case, why had she made EllaBelle all those beautiful dresses? And what could EllaBelle possibly have done to merit such disapproval? She had been dead for more than two years, but Buddy remembered her well enough to know that she'd been a warm, funny, delightful kind of mother.

Her eyes stung. She needed a tissue and couldn't remember where there were any.

In the kitchen, the light went out as Cassie, too, left the room. She walked past Buddy's doorway in the dark, no doubt knowing every foot of the house by heart after living here all of her life. Buddy waited to venture out for her glass of water until she heard the stairs creak for the last time as her aunt went up.

She didn't turn on a light, either. She didn't want to alert anyone to the fact that she'd been listening to all of that. It wasn't pitch-black. There was a yard light somewhere that penetrated the house enough to keep Buddy from running into anything, as long as she walked carefully and felt her way.

*Oh, Daddy,* she thought mournfully, *where are you? Why don't you come get me? I want to go home!*

But there was no home. And something truly terrible must have happened to her father to have kept him away from her.

Tears were running down her face as she finally reached the kitchen sink and found a glass in the cupboard overhead. The running water sounded loud—loud enough to be heard upstairs? She drank one glass quickly, and then filled it again.

In the room behind her, Grandpa activated the clock. "The time is 11:05 P.M.," the tinny voice recited.

Buddy made her way back to bed and lay there with trembling lips as she repeated her prayers for her father and for Bart. And she decided that maybe Addie had exaggerated a little, that while Grandpa didn't push the button on his clock every thirty seconds, he most assuredly did it ten or twelve times over every half hour.

She finally fell asleep in spite of that nasty little speaking clock, and woke to the smell of bacon cooking and coffee perking, and the sound of the clock announcing the time. "8:36 A.M.," it said, and she supposed she'd better get up and get dressed. While she was pulling on her jeans and sweatshirt, Buddy prayed that Cassie would take Addie's advice and not invite *her* to help take Gus to get his head X-rayed.

And she continued to feel completely bewildered about a reference to money that was gone.

# 8

"Ouch!" Cassie exclaimed as Buddy walked into the kitchen. "I'd forgotten how often you get burned, frying bacon on top of the stove. I suppose we won't dare ask Gordon to replace the microwave and the remote control right away, will we?"

Addie sipped at her coffee, obviously having otherwise finished her breakfast. "No, we won't. Not when he's just sent us the money for four new tires. We used to be able to get along without a microwave and a remote. We'll just have to learn to do it again."

"I don't mind getting up to change channels. But we used the microwave so much."

Grandpa wandered in from his room, heading past them toward the dining room. "I'm cold," he announced. "I'm going to turn up the heat."

"No, Grandpa," Addie said, standing up and blocking his way. "It's already plenty warm enough in here for everybody else. Put on your sweater and you'll be fine."

He stared at her crossly. "I don't know where my sweater is."

"Well, I'm sure Buddy will be glad to help you find it." She turned toward Buddy. "He probably dropped it in his rocker, that's where it usually is. It's bright blue, so he can see it more easily. He can still detect color quite well if he wants to, in his peripheral vision."

Buddy nodded and headed for Grandpa's room as his clock chimed out the time again. The sweater was right where Addie had said it would be, so she brought it back with her. Grandpa looked a bit surly, but he did put it on.

"I have to go," Addie said, picking up her purse. She was looking quite smart in a dark suit with a white blouse and a bright printed scarf. "See you at suppertime."

Cassie forked bacon onto a plate covered with paper towels. "Run upstairs, would you, Buddy, and tell Max that breakfast is ready? Usually he smells bacon and comes on the double."

"All right," Buddy agreed, and wondered who had done all the little errands when she wasn't there. She returned a few minutes later with her report. "He's not in his room."

Cassie hesitated with bread ready to drop into the toaster. "Was his bed made?"

"No."

"He must have gotten up and left before I was up. Now why did he go and do that?"

*Because he didn't want to see anybody,* Buddy thought. *Not his father, not Cassie. And maybe he doesn't intend to do the chores Gus told him to do this morning.*

Cassie sighed. "I was counting on him to help me get Gus down to the car when we're ready to go."

*Another reason to disappear,* Buddy thought. She held her breath, waiting for Cassie's request for her own help. It came, but not in helping with Gus.

"I hope you won't mind looking after Grandpa while we're gone. As soon as I've finished here I'll hide the knobs again so he can't use the range. You can get them down if you need to warm up some soup for him. Or he can just have a sandwich. He likes peaches. You might open a jar. The pantry's full of canned stuff."

A relieved breath slid out of her as Buddy agreed. Looking after Grandpa seemed an easier task than anything to do with Gus.

"I've put corned beef and cabbage in the Crock-Pot for supper," Cassie said, loading a plate and carrying it to set before Buddy at the table. "You don't have to do anything with that. I need to get the car over to the garage to have the tires put on. I'll be back as soon as I can. I just have to carry this other plate up to Gus. He didn't want to come down to breakfast."

Buddy didn't know all that much about alcoholics, being lucky enough not to have known any personally. But she guessed that having been drunk enough to fall down and cut his head open last night probably meant that Gus would have a hangover headache this morning.

"Don't I get any breakfast?" Grandpa asked.

"You already had some, honey," Cassie told him. "Bacon and pancakes, remember? Would you like a doughnut and another cup of coffee?"

So Buddy and Grandpa ate breakfast together, her first and his second. Before the meal was over, he had activated his hanging clock seven times.

Cassie came back down with Gus's tray as it sounded the last time. "I hope that didn't keep you awake last night," she said.

"I heard it a few times," Buddy admitted.

"It drives Addie crazy. But since he can't see anymore, can't read, can't work in the garden, it seems to be the only thing that keeps him oriented to where he is and what's supposed to be going on. He needs to know what time it is."

Buddy nodded. It was disconcerting, the way everybody discussed Grandpa as if he weren't there, even when she realized that he probably wasn't hearing very much of it.

Cassie had a purse ready, too, and keys in her hand. "If Max comes back, would you remind him about mowing the lawn? Gus will be annoyed if he doesn't do it."

Buddy hesitated, mopping up the last of the maple syrup with a bite of pancake. "What kind of mower do you have? I used to help Bart sometimes. Maybe I could do it."

Cassie brightened. "Do you think so? I used to do it, before I married Gus and Max came to live here. Come along with me and I'll show you."

The power mower wasn't exactly like the one stored in the garage at the old house, but they got it up and running, and by the time Cassie had backed the car out onto the street, Buddy was cutting the first swath across the side of the lot. She rather enjoyed doing it, and was finished by the time the new tires had been put on. She was in the back hall, tying up bundles of old newspapers, when she heard Cassie and Gus leave the house, with him protesting that he didn't want to go, and Cassie insisting.

There was an old wagon in the garage. She loaded the newspapers into it and hoped Max would come back in time to tell her where to take them for recycling. Now it was time, she figured, to check on Grandpa.

He had obviously turned up the heat, for the house was sweltering. She went into the dining room and adjusted the temperature downward, noting that someone had put duct tape and a small wooden guard on the thermostat so that it couldn't be pushed above eighty degrees.

It wasn't hard to find him; all she had to do was follow the speaking clock. He was in the kitchen, punching futilely at the numbers on the micro-wave. "It won't work," he announced as she entered.

"No," Buddy agreed. "Can I heat something for you on the stove?"

"There's no way to turn it on. All the knobs are missing."

"How about a sandwich? And Aunt Cassie said I could open some peaches, from the pantry."

He was easily diverted. "A sandwich and peaches. That sounds good." He tilted his head, presumably so he was looking at her through the part of his eye where there was still vision. "Do I know you, Sister?"

"I'm Buddy. EllaBelle's daughter."

"Oh, yes. I thought you seemed familiar. Your voice . . . I remember your voice."

Buddy stepped over beside him and opened the ruined microwave with its blackened interior walls. There was a cup of coffee in it, and she took it out. If she'd caught his movements accurately, he had tried to set the timer for thirty minutes, long enough to have boiled the coffee over and possibly damaged the oven again if it had been functioning.

"How about a glass of milk instead of this? Okay?"

"Okay," Grandpa agreed. "Where's Sister?"

"Aunt Cassie's gone to Kalispell. Aunt Addie's at the library." She opened the bread box and started getting out fixings for the sandwich. Tuna fish with mayonnaise, she decided, since that was what she spotted in the refrigerator.

"Umm. I used to go to the library at least once a week," he told her, moving toward the table, poking ahead with his cane. "I can't read anymore. Not even the Good Book. I memorized a lot of that, though, and it's still stuck in my head. But I can't read novels. Mysteries, or Westerns. I don't like those science fiction things about all those spaceships and aliens, do you?"

"Yes, I like those. Do you want chopped pickles?"

"Yes, pickles are good. What about the peaches?"

Buddy found them in the pantry, row after row of home-canned fruits and vegetables. She made a nice lunch for the two of them, and they ate in a companionable silence, for the most part, though occasionally Grandpa would make an intriguing remark. "Sister writes novels, I think. I don't believe I've read any of them."

And that reminded Buddy that she and Grandpa were the only ones in the house, and that Addie's rooms upstairs held not only a manuscript that had been returned, but a photograph album that had old family pictures she hadn't seen.

After Grandpa had had two dishes of peaches, he wiped his mouth with a paper napkin and pushed back his chair. "I think I'll take a nap now," he said. "I wish Blackie would come and sleep by my feet. Do you know where he is?"

"Not exactly," Buddy replied, hoping he wouldn't press any further. It must be terrible not to remember that you'd been told that your pet had died, so that you felt the sorrow all over again each time.

She heard the talking clock several times while she was clearing the table and wiping off the counter, and then there was only silence. The big house seemed to be waiting for her to do something.

She knew it wasn't right to pry into anyone else's belongings. Yet there was a picture of her father in that photo album on Addie's dresser. A picture she had never seen before yesterday, one that demanded an explanation, though it was unlikely anyone would provide it.

She walked quietly up the stairway—hearing the squeak of that one loose step—and stood in the doorway of Addie's bedroom.

The door was open, and across the room she could see the photograph album, in plain sight.

What harm would it do to look at old pictures, taken years before?

It wasn't only that snapshot, of course. There were the things she'd overheard her aunts and her great-grandfather say. "It's not fair to hold . . . the way you feel about EllaBelle . . . against Buddy. She can't help what her mother did." And, "I got out the clothes, with a painful memory in every stitch I had put into every dress. . . . I'm reminded of difficult things when I look at Buddy, . . ." Addie had said. Because Buddy looked like her mother, was the implication. And, "I don't blame her for the money being gone." How could she find out what all that meant?

And Grandpa had said, "Sister cried when Ella-Belle ran off and married Dan Adams." *Which sister had cried, Addie or Cassie? And why?*

Hesitating, Buddy looked around Addie's room. It was large and sunny and full of shelves of books and pictures and objects Addie had collected over the years. A beautiful pale pink shell. A devotional book, lying flat with a purple ribbon marking a place. Photos, including one of her mother in a graduation cap and gown.

Why was she keeping that, in plain sight, if she felt EllaBelle had done something wrong? Something to hurt her? Was Addie the sister who had cried when EllaBelle had eloped?

There was nothing in the room to suggest that Addie had lived here with a husband, nor that she had retained things from her own girlhood. This was a woman's room, where Addie lived alone.

What had she said about Uncle Ed? "At least Ed had the decency to die on me." Did that mean it was a relief that he was gone?

Buddy thought about Gus, and wondered if Cassie would find it a relief if *he* were to die. Even his own son had expressed the hope that he'd fall and break his neck. Buddy couldn't imagine thinking anything like that about her father.

And when they had mentioned the fact that Grandpa had sold the store that had supported his family for so many years, they'd said something about cash. A whole bagful of cash, hadn't Grandpa said that?

If he had a lot of money, why did they have to depend on Uncle Gordon to buy tires for the car, and why weren't they able to replace the microwave and the remote control? Was it Grandpa's money Addie had referred to as being gone? If so, what had happened to it?

There was a miniature cedar chest on the far end of the dresser. Buddy reached over and lifted the lid, expecting to see the same kind of odds and ends her mother had kept in one just like it. But there were no souvenirs of high school proms, no pressed flowers, no sentimental notes, no jewelry.

There were folded handkerchiefs, smelling faintly of cedar, and a small blue bank book.

Buddy flipped open the cover and saw that it was

an account that had been started many years ago. Addie had put small amounts into it, and taken small amounts out from time to time, and the balance right now was less than one hundred dollars.

Feeling guilty, Buddy closed the lid.

The return envelope from the publishing company lay where she had last seen it. It was still sealed, as if Addie had not been able to bring herself to open it and read the rejection letter it contained.

Of course the photographs and snapshots were what she'd come to look at. She picked up the album, listening to the silence of the house. There was no reason to think she had to hurry. Neither of her aunts would be coming home to surprise her in this room where she had no right to be.

She carried the big book over to sit in the rocking chair at the foot of the bed, and opened it on her lap.

The picture of her father and Addie, taken so long ago, was just as she'd left it earlier. This time she studied it more closely, then turned it over to see what was written on the back. DAN AND ME, was all it said, FOURTH OF JULY.

No date.

Slowly Buddy leafed through the album, as she had done with the one belonging to her mother. There was nothing out of the ordinary about it. Snapshots of a family, three sisters and a brother,

108

with parents and grandparents and an occasional pet mixed in.

It told her nothing except that her father and Addie had been friends. They had had their pictures taken together at least half a dozen times. There was no snapshot of Dan and EllaBelle together.

Somewhere in the house was a sound that brought her upright, heart pounding. She had learned nothing, and now she would feel guilty forever, snooping this way. But how else did a kid find out anything important, without snooping?

She replaced the album where it belonged and went back downstairs, trying to think of an excuse for having gone up there if she got caught. She had no legitimate excuse for being upstairs.

It must have been just the creaking of the old house, she decided. There was no one around. Not even Grandpa's talking clock marred the silence.

In the kitchen the aroma of corned beef and cabbage drifted from the Crock-Pot. She wondered if they'd keep Gus at the hospital if he *did* have a more serious injury than Addie had thought, or if she'd have to sit through another of those uncomfortable meals with Max's father present tonight.

Max came through the back door as she was trying to decide what to do next. She wished Bart would call with an update—had he talked to anyone yet who had seen Dad or his truck? But of course not. He'd let her know when there was any news. He knew how worried she was.

Max was wearing a blue jacket and a baseball cap, and he pulled the kitten out of the jacket front as he entered the house.

"Who mowed the lawn?" he demanded, putting the animal down near his bowl and getting out what was left of the tuna for him. Apparently Scamp didn't object to pickles and mayonnaise, because he ate greedily.

"I did. The mower is almost like ours at home," Buddy said, before she remembered that she no longer had a home.

"You tie up the newspapers, too?" He'd noticed the wagon load near the back steps.

"I didn't know where to take them," Buddy said.

"Come on, I'll show you where the recycling place is. It's just a big bin, behind the grocery store."

"I'm supposed to be watching over Grandpa," Buddy said. "He's taking a nap."

"He usually sleeps for a couple of hours in the afternoon. Just like a baby," Max said. "We can be back before he wakes up."

She wasn't sure that was the proper way to watch over the old man, but she did want to get back out in the sunshine. "Okay," she agreed, and was glad Max pulled the wagon and didn't expect her to do it.

They were on the way back when she finally asked the question that had been on her tongue for some time. Her mouth felt dry, and she didn't know if he'd answer or not. "They said Grandpa sold his store for a lot of money. Cash, he said. A whole bagful of cash."

"Yeah, I guess it was thousands of dollars. They were all mad at him for demanding it in cash instead of a check to put in the bank. That way, it probably wouldn't have disappeared."

Buddy paused on the sidewalk to take that in. "It disappeared? Don't they know what happened to it?"

He stared at her in surprise. "Yeah. Didn't you know? Your mother stole it."

# 9

Buddy staggered as if she'd been kicked in the stomach. "That's a lie!" she exclaimed when she could speak. "My mom never stole anything in her life!"

Max shrugged. "I wasn't here when it happened. I just heard about it. They talk about it when they don't know I'm listening. For once, I don't think the whole town knows, but I've heard it plenty of times."

"Then you must have heard wrong!"

Max started walking again, pulling the empty wagon. Buddy wasn't sure she had the strength to walk with him. She felt outraged, sick, disbelieving at his accusation.

"All I know is that as long as Grandpa had money, they seemed to be able to do the things they wanted. While he ran the store I don't think they bought a lot of stuff, but they could fix anything that broke, at least. Then, after the money disappeared, they couldn't afford it. Cassie doesn't have any income of her own, except for what their father left her and Addie. It pays the taxes and basic expenses, but there isn't much left over. At least it makes it possible for her to stay here and look after Grandpa. He has Social Security, but that's not very much, either. And Addie has a small salary from the job at the library, and once in a while a small check for an article she sells to a magazine. And Pa—"

A bitter spasm twisted Max's face. "He's got a pension because he hurt his back and can't work. But he spends a lot of time over at the Hayloft. He even buys drinks for other guys sometimes. We would just barely survive if we didn't live here, in Grandpa's house, which will belong to Cassie and Addie when he dies. It's been paid for years, so that part doesn't cost anything. Once in a while my mom sends a check to use for me. School clothes, things like that. But I don't always get it the way I'm supposed to, unless Cassie insists. I always make sure she knows when it comes."

He didn't state where the money from his mother went, but when Buddy's mind began to work again, she made a good guess. Gus treated more friends at the tavern.

"You're sure they said my mom took the money? You mean Addie and Cassie said so?"

It would explain why Addie felt resentment against her younger sister, if it were true. But how could it be true? "Mama was the most honest person alive," she said stubbornly.

Max kicked a small rock off the sidewalk as they reached the house and took the wagon back to the garage. "All I know is what I hear," he said.

"And this is what Addie holds against Mama? That she thinks Mama stole money from Grandpa? Money that would have helped support them all, and keep the house up?"

She sounded angry, and Max dropped the handle of the wagon and held up his hands. "Hey, don't shoot the messenger, okay? You asked me, and I told you what I know. I didn't make up the news. I just know what I hear them all saying, you know?"

"I'd never have come here if I'd known this," Buddy said.

"I wouldn't have come here, either, if I could have helped it," Max said as they walked from the garage to the house. "Though living with Pa in two rooms over Mallory's garage wasn't great. This is better, in many ways. Cassie means well. So does Addie, I guess. And I don't mind Grandpa. When his mind isn't wandering, he's kind of a neat old guy. Get him talking about the old days that he still remembers and he can tell some terrific stories."

As they went up the back steps together, Max shot her a look. "Did your dad leave you a note when he went away?"

"A note?" She was momentarily distracted from the accusation against her mother. "No, why would he leave a note? We were all together at home, and he told us what to do, and Rich picked him up right in front. He told me to mind Bart and said he'd be back in week or so and we'd all go out for steaks or pizza, whichever we wanted. He hugged us and got in Rich's car and waved good-bye, and that was all."

Max held open the screen door for her. "My mom left a note. We didn't get a chance to say good-bye. She was sorry she couldn't take me with her, because she didn't have any money and didn't know how she was going to manage, but she said she'd write later."

"And did she?"

"Yeah, about once a month. Says she misses me." Max wiped the back of a hand across his mouth. "I know she feels bad that I have to live with Pa, when she couldn't. She explained it to me. Said he was an alcoholic and would never change, and she couldn't stand it any longer. But I'm still stuck with him. Whew! Grandpa's been at the thermostat again!"

The house was very hot. They heard the talking clock, and found Grandpa standing before the thermostat in the dining room. He heard them coming and gave them a triumphant grin.

"Somebody stuck this junk all over it so I couldn't turn it up any higher, but I got it all off," he told them, holding the wads of duct tape and the little wedge of wood that had limited the settings.

Max held out his hand for the stuff. "Sorry, Grandpa, but I'm going to have to put them back on. If it gets too hot, nobody else can breathe in here, and they're afraid you'll burn the house down. Come on, let's go get your sweater, okay?"

"I wouldn't burn anything down," the old man protested, though he allowed himself to be steered out of the dining room. "I used to put out fires, you know. I was on the volunteer fire department for years. If there wasn't anybody to look after the store, I'd lock it up and jump in my pickup and off I'd go, whenever the whistle blew. We had signals in those days, you know. No CBs in people's trucks. One blast was for the north side of town. Two meant south. Three was east, and four toots meant we headed west. We always found the fire, following the pumper truck and the siren, and most of the time we put it out."

He obediently held out an arm for his sweater when Max fetched it for him. "I always made a donation for the fire department when they asked. Did I make my donation yet this year?"

"I don't think so," Max told him. "Man, it's broiling in here. You want a cold drink?" He peered into the refrigerator. "Which do you want?"

"Orange," Grandpa decided. Buddy and Max settled for grape, and Max handed out the cans.

"How come I didn't make a donation yet? The fire department's a worthy cause," Grandpa said as they took chairs around the table.

"I don't think you've got any money, Grandpa," Max told him, sliding a glance toward Buddy to see if she was going to erupt again.

The old man frowned. "I used to have money. A lot of money. Filled up a whole bag with cash."

"Yeah, well, it's gone now," Max informed him. "You should have put it in the bank instead of keeping it at home."

Grandpa was still scowling. "Don't trust banks. They all failed."

"That was many years ago, Grandpa," Max assured him. "The banks are all right now. You should have just let old Peterson write you a check, and put it in the bank."

"Alf Peterson. Never trusted him. He wrote bad checks. I remember. I didn't trust him to pay for the store with a check, so I insisted on cash. There was a whole lot of it. The banker didn't want him to have that much in cash, but I insisted.

It was *my* money. Alf bought a car from me once and the check bounced and I had a terrible time getting my money out of him. Couldn't trust him as far as I could have thrown him."

Buddy's mouth had gotten drier and drier in spite of the grape soda. "Why did you think Mama took your cash money?"

Shock flashed across Max's face, but Grandpa's look turned puzzled. "Your mama? Did I say your mama took my money?"

"EllaBelle was my mother." Buddy pushed forward, determined to know more than Max had told her. "Max says Aunt Addie and Aunt Cassie both think she stole your money."

"I never said that, did I?" He scratched his head thoughtfully. "I don't remember saying that. I just put it somewhere safe, didn't I?"

Buddy leaned forward on her elbows. "Where? Where was it safe?"

"I don't know," the old man said after a moment during which he thought hard. "I have a little trouble with my memory these days, you know. Can't always remember everything, the way I used to. Don't worry. It'll turn up one of these days."

"After two and a half years?" Max muttered under his breath.

"But you don't think EllaBelle stole it?" Buddy asked hopefully.

"EllaBelle was a nice little girl. Prettiest one of the

bunch, wasn't she? All those curls." He squinted at Buddy. "You don't have curls, do you?"

"No. I can't believe she stole your money, Grandpa."

"No. I can't, either. I used to feed her butter-scotch drops. Grandma scolded me for giving all the youngsters candy, but I can't see that it hurt them any. Didn't spoil their appetites much, and I always told them to brush their teeth afterward. Do you brush regularly?"

Buddy was getting that down-the-rabbit-hole feeling again.

What had she learned today? Several things, none of them trustworthy. There was no way she'd ever be convinced that her mother had been a thief. She looked at Max. Surely he, too, could see that not everything he'd heard was necessarily true.

Max wiggled his eyebrows, signaling his own bafflement.

"Why do grown-ups talk in riddles instead of saying the truth straight out?" Buddy asked in frustration.

"I try to say the truth straight out," Grandpa asserted. "Always have. Good business. People trust you."

Max laughed. "You're one of us kids, Grandpa," he said, and drained his can of pop as he stood up. "I better go find another stick of wood and fix that thermostat before anybody else gets home.

They get upset when he undoes their traps or their tricks."

Grandpa turned to follow his movements. "What's he going to do?"

"Fix the thermostat," Buddy told him, flinching at her own evasive response after she'd just wished that people would speak more plainly.

"Good. Good. It needs fixing. It was broken, so I couldn't turn it up," Grandpa said. "Is it suppertime yet?" He punched the button on his clock and got the time. "Have we had supper yet?"

"No, Grandpa. But it's cooking. We'll eat when Aunt Cassie and Aunt Addie come home."

"Good girls," Grandpa approved. "Always been really good to me. Take care of me. Kind of bossy, though, sometimes."

Max was right, Buddy thought. Addie and Cassie were the grown-ups, and she and Max and Grandpa were the kids. They were the ones who didn't have anything to say about what they had to do.

And what would happen if Bart didn't find Dad? Sorrow rushed through her, making her ache with an almost physical pain. Bart had to find him, she thought, determined not to give in to despair. But it was getting harder all the time.

Gus had a concussion, but he didn't have to stay in the hospital in Kalispell. The doctor said he could recuperate just as well at home. Buddy got the impression that the trip had not been a particularly pleasant one. Gus was grumpy and said he was going to lie down again, and Cassie was clearly worn out.

She checked on the Crock-Pot, and thanked Buddy for keeping an eye on Grandpa. "I hope he wasn't too much trouble."

"No trouble at all," Buddy said, deciding not to mention the altered thermostat and the answers Grandpa had given to her questions. She wanted to press the issue of Mama's stealing Grandpa's money, but didn't quite dare. Maybe when Bart and Dad showed up, and they were ready to leave, she would be brave enough to confront her aunts about it, but not now. Not while she still had to live here, under their supervision. ·

She wondered if her father had any idea what they thought, and could not believe that he did. *Oh, Daddy, please come back! Please be safe,* she begged silently. *Please let us be a normal family again.*

She could hardly believe that it would ever happen, yet she refused to give up hope. *Soon, soon there will be another phone call from my brother, and it will be all right. She had to believe that, or her heart would truly break.*

# 10

Buddy's second night in the old house wasn't nearly as disrupted as the first one. She kept hearing Grandpa's talking clock, but somehow it didn't bother her as much as it had the previous night. It helped to know that it was his way of orienting himself in a world where so much was beyond his ability to see or understand or remember.

And he did remember her mother with fondness. He didn't think EllaBelle had stolen his money.

There were no explosions, no late-night overheard conversations, nothing further to upset her.

The only thing making her uneasy on Sunday morning, except for worrying about Dad and Bart, was the idea of going to church in a town where everyone had known her entire family all their lives. Probably some of them thought her mother had stolen money from Grandpa, though Max said he didn't think Addie and Cassie had talked about it. Still, Buddy had lived in a number of small towns like this, and it always seemed that if you so much as spit on the sidewalk, the word got back to your folks before you had time to get home.

The phone didn't ring. No report from her brother. Grandpa had to be bullied into taking a shower, which he insisted he didn't need, and there was a brief interlude during which the old man thought Blackie was back.

"No, Grandpa," Max said firmly. "This isn't Blackie. Blackie got hit by a car a long time ago. This is Scamp. See, he's a different color. And he's *my* cat."

Gus, it became apparent, did not join the family at church. They didn't take the car; they walked. It was only three blocks. And just as Buddy had feared, it seemed that the entire town was there.

Cassie had allowed plenty of time to get there and greet all their neighbors before the service began.

The ladies all approached, smiling, or, in a few cases, not smiling. "EllaBelle's girl," they said. "Looks just like her." "How do you like it here in Haysville, dear?" Or, "Buddy? They call you Buddy?"

Buddy had begun to wonder how she could manage to get rid of that nickname. She didn't like the way people reacted to it, when their eyebrows and their voices went up upon hearing it.

It was a relief when the organ began to play, and they went inside the old white frame church with the steeple atop it, and found places in one of the long pews. Max, along under pressure, escaped to sit with some friends up in the balcony. Buddy found herself sandwiched between Addie and Grandpa, with Cassie beyond him.

"If he sings too loud," Addie whispered, "stick your elbow in his ribs."

He *did* sing very loudly, but he sang on-key, and he knew the words to all the hymns without having to be able to read them in the book. Buddy didn't poke him. She rather enjoyed it when he belted out, "'When the roll is called up yonder, I'll be there.'"

On the way out after the sermon, the pastor shook Grandpa's hand and said with a smile, "You were in fine voice this morning, Harry."

"Cassie says the Lord's not deaf, so I don't need to shout. But I want to be sure He hears me."

The pastor laughed and reached for Buddy's hand. "Good to have you with us, young lady. I hope you're enjoying your visit."

She couldn't quite bring herself to murmur just

how much she was enjoying it, but she thanked him and walked gratefully out into the sunshine.

The school principal, Herbert Faulkner, spoke to her, too. "Be looking forward to seeing you tomorrow morning, Amy Kate," he said.

She couldn't come up with an appropriate response to that, either. She was praying that before then Bart would call and say he and Dad were on their way here, and there'd be no need for her to start school in Haysville.

They walked home slowly, Cassie and Addie ahead, Buddy and Grandpa behind. Max had gone on ahead. The old man leaned on his cane, but he was otherwise quite sprightly. "Good sermon," he said. "I always enjoy a good sermon."

"Especially when it's not aimed at you," Addie said.

"It was aimed at Gus, I think. But he wasn't there, was he? I'll have to tell him about it," Grandpa offered.

Startled, Buddy wondered if he'd remember until they got home, and what Gus would think of being listed among the sinners. It probably wouldn't improve Gus's disposition, though it rather tickled her that Grandpa was sharp enough to grasp the point of the sermon.

"Saw Jack Cline," Grandpa went on. "Told him I thought he was dead. But he said, No, he was quite alive. Just been on a trip to Florida. Tampa, I believe."

Max met them at the door when they got home. "There was a phone call for Buddy, I think. The Caller ID didn't give his name, or hers, but it came from a pay phone in Willits, California. I figured your brother was maybe there, looking for your dad."

Anguish rushed through Buddy's chest. Bart had called, and she'd missed him! Oh, why hadn't she insisted on staying at home, just in case? Now she didn't know if he had news or not, if it was good or bad—

"He'll call back," Addie said, seeing her face.

But it was Addie who thought her father was unreliable, that he couldn't be trusted to keep his promise to come back for his children.

It was all Buddy could do to keep from crying in disappointment.

"I can smell dinner cooking," Cassie said. "I'd better check the oven before I go up and change my clothes."

"Do I have to change my clothes?" Grandpa wanted to know as he and Addie followed Cassie toward the back of the house. "I remember my mother always made me change my clothes the minute I got home from school so I wouldn't get my good ones dirty."

"Most people don't bother with that anymore," Addie was telling him as they walked out of sight. "They just wash load after load in their automatic washers."

"I used to sell automatic washing machines. Didn't I?"

Buddy wasn't listening. She stared at the telephone, willing it to ring again with Bart calling back, but it didn't.

"Uh . . . ," Max said, clearing his throat.

Buddy looked at him.

"Uh, Pa's in kind of a bad mood today. Worse than usual," he said. "He, uh, he said it was a good thing I did the chores he told me to do yesterday. You know, cutting the grass. And taking the newspapers to be recycled. And I"—he cleared his throat again, and blushed—"I didn't tell him you did it. I let him think—"

"That's okay." Buddy shrugged. "It doesn't matter."

He hesitated, then said, "Thanks. I guess I'm a coward, but when he's off his feed, he's . . . hard to deal with. When we lived with my mom, she wouldn't let him pick on me, but that meant they were always fighting. Cassie never fights with him, but she doesn't always take my side in an argument, either, except to make sure I get the benefit of the money my mom sends. Did your folks fight?"

"Not very often. Hardly ever. Cassie seems nice, though. It seems funny that she's your stepmother. You like her, don't you?"

"Cassie?" He made a face that she couldn't quite interpret. "Yeah, I guess. It's better living with her than with only Pa. And she cooks good. But she's what my mom calls an *enabler*."

Buddy allowed herself to be distracted from her disappointment about missing Bart's call. "What's that mean?"

"It means she doesn't do anything wrong herself—like drink too much and fall down, or be mean to other people—but she makes it possible for Pa to keep on doing those things. My mom couldn't make him stop, so she left, see? She wouldn't let him keep his beer in the house. She tried to insist that he take the responsibility for paying the rent and buying the groceries. She didn't try to find other ways to take care of those things so Pa could just coast, the way he does here. She didn't make excuses for him. She didn't make it easier for him to skip the responsibility part of marriage, the way Cassie does."

"An enabler," Buddy repeated. "Someone who . . . who enables someone else to do something he shouldn't be allowed to do."

"Right. Mom said she felt guilty leaving me behind, but without money or a job or a place to stay, she couldn't take me along. She couldn't even guarantee that we'd both have enough to eat. But she promised that someday she'd get me back, when she could take care of me." Max bit his lip. "Do you believe in someday?"

Buddy didn't have to think about that for very

long. "Yes. Someday she'll come back for you, and someday—soon—my dad will come back for my brother and me."

This wasn't the time to admit how scared she was that something terrible had happened to her father, that he might not be *able* to return.

"I'm twelve," Max said. "When I'm eighteen, and out of school, I'll get a job and take care of *her,* if I need to."

*Six years,* Buddy thought. That was a long time.

Yet not as long as it would be for her if Bart didn't find Dad, if the two of them didn't come back together.

Beside them, the phone rang.

Max grabbed it. "Yeah? I mean, hello? Yes, she's right here."

"Bart?" Buddy asked eagerly, taking the phone from Max.

"Yeah, it's me. Listen, I found somebody who saw Dad. Four days ago. She's a waitress in a little restaurant on Highway 101. She even remembered what he had to eat. Two hamburgers with everything, fries, and an order of onion rings. And she filled his Thermos with coffee. She didn't see Rich, but she said Dad told her his partner was in the sleeper, and he took him a ham sandwich and a piece of cherry pie. Remember how Rich always liked cherry pie?"

"Yes. So she was sure it really was Dad? Does

she know what happened to him?" Buddy's chest was tight again, barely allowing her to breathe. "Was he all right then?"

"He was fine. She said he was cheerful, mentioned that he had a new job and that he had two kids at home, and that they'd probably have to move as soon as he got a couple of paychecks so that he could afford it."

"Then where is he?" Buddy begged. "How could he just disappear with an eighteen-wheeler?"

"I don't know yet. She said he kept trying to use the phone, but some guy was hogging it and he finally gave up and said he'd try farther down the line. But I know he got this far, heading south. I thought you'd want to know that I had some definite word, and a time when he was here. So I'm taking it slow, driving in the direction he was going. I'm stopping everywhere I think he could have stopped. For fuel, for food. I've got his picture with me, that one of him we took last summer at the beach, and this waitress recognized it right away. Maybe somebody else will, too." Bart hesitated. "You doing okay, Buddy?"

She thought of the way Addie had spoken about their father, and what it was like being in the middle of a dysfunctional family, and having to go to school in Haysville tomorrow with a bunch of strangers, and of Grandpa blowing up the microwave and the remote control, and knew this wasn't the time to tell Bart about any of that. "I'm okay," she said. "Call me again the minute you learn anything else, will you? Promise?"

"Promise," Bart assured her. "I miss you, Buddy."

"I miss you, too," she said, feeling the sting of tears. "Good luck, Bart. Keeping looking until you find him."

"I will," he said, and then he was gone.

"He didn't find your dad yet," Max said as she slowly replaced the receiver.

"No, but he found a waitress who remembered seeing him. He's getting closer."

"He'll probably find him tomorrow, maybe, then."

She didn't know if that was true or not, but she was grateful to Max for helping her hang on to the hope.

Max inhaled deeply. "Smells like the chicken must be close to done. Cassie makes great dressing to stuff a chicken. At least Pa married somebody who keeps us fed, even if he doesn't pay for much of it."

They heard Grandpa's voice raised querulously in the kitchen. "Somebody must have taken them. I know I left them on my dresser, where I always kept them."

As they walked into the room, Cassie was dishing up mashed potatoes. There were two golden brown roasting hens resting on twin platters on the counter. "Max, would you call Gus, please? It's all ready to eat right now."

"Why did somebody take my pills?" Grandpa demanded, paying no attention to what Cassie was saying. "My hip is hurting, and I need the pills."

"I'll get you the pills, Grandpa," Addie assured him. "I put them away so you wouldn't take too many of them like you did the last time your arthritis kicked up."

"It always hurts when it's going to rain. I want the pills where I can take them when I need them."

"I have to keep them, because when they're on your dresser, you take too many of them all at once. That's not safe. Just tell me when you need them," Addie said, and disappeared into the hall-way to the ground-floor bathroom. She returned with a small bottle and dumped several pills into his outstretched hand.

Grandpa was not mollified. He was still angry that Addie had taken them. "I've been taking my own pills all my life—over ninety years, isn't it?—and I don't need somebody else to tell me when I need them."

"You need someone to keep you from overdos-ing," Addie said calmly. "The last time you had a bad spell, you took thirty capsules in one day. That could make you very sick, or even kill you."

"You're treating me as if I were a child," Grandpa said. "This is still my house, and I'm old enough to know when I need a pain pill."

"It's just that you forget how many you've taken, honey," Cassie soothed. "Take those, and you'll feel better soon. Max, haven't you gone after your father yet? The food's going to get cold. Sit down, Grandpa. Buddy, would you dish up those green beans in that blue bowl, please?"

Five minutes after they'd said grace and commenced to eat, Grandpa suddenly blurted into the middle of a conversation about who they'd talked to at church, "You should have been at services, Gus. The pastor gave an excellent sermon about the evils of drink."

Gus glared at him. "Don't bother telling me about it. I've already heard it. Pass the butter, Max."

"I'll have some, too," Cassie requested.

That was enough to get them off the subject for a few minutes, and then Grandpa said, "My hip aches. I need a pain pill. Those red and yellow ones."

"You just took two of them ten minutes ago," Addie said. "Wait a little longer, and they'll start to work."

Buddy, savoring roasted chicken and mashed potatoes and gravy and biscuits, thought of how much more fun it was to eat with Dad and Bart, even if they weren't eating such a delicious meal. Everybody would be laughing, not squabbling. But she felt sorry for Grandpa. It must be awful not to remember things any longer than he did. She could see how he'd make a mistake and take too many pills, when he couldn't remember that he'd already taken some, and she understood why Addie had taken them away and hidden them. But she longed for a more normal household, with no grumpy Gus eating in his undershirt, no Max sunk in silence after his father had chewed him out for not remembering to bring in the Sunday paper before he went off to church.

After dinner, which was capped off by apple crisp and ice cream, the adults all decided they were in need of naps. It was hard to understand how Gus could need one, since he hadn't even gotten out of bed until the others got home, but as long as he went away, Buddy was happy to have him go back to sleep.

She didn't feel any need of a nap. She decided to finish the book about the family whose lives had been disrupted by a bear, and retired to the little sewing room.

Later she was aware of the reawakening of the household; there were sounds, voices, the slamming of a door. Then Max stood in her own doorway. "Have you seen Grandpa?" he asked.

Buddy set her book aside. "Not since we ate dinner."

"He seems to have disappeared," Max said. "Nobody can find him. I think they want us all to look for him."

# 11

They began to look for Grandpa around four in the afternoon.

They checked out the entire house first, of course, including the attic. Because her legs were younger, Buddy got to climb up there. The stairs were so narrow and so steep, she didn't wonder they hadn't tried to haul the stuff from the sewing room and Addie's back bedroom office up there. It was so packed with junk, there wasn't room for much more, anyway. The result, she decided, of the family's having lived in one place for so long. There was no sign of Grandpa, and the search moved outside.

At first nobody panicked. Since the old man saw so poorly, nobody thought he would have wandered far from the house. But after an hour, when there was still no clue as to his whereabouts, they broadened the base of their operations.

"Max, you go toward town and ask, house to house, if anyone has seen him," Addie directed, and her voice had become sharp with anxiety. "I'll take the other end of the street. Cassie can take the car and head over toward the school, and then the church. Gus—"

Gus grunted a denial. "Don't assign anything to me. I'm not feeling well enough to go out and walk up and down for blocks. I'll stay here in case there's any news on the phone."

"What shall I do?" Buddy asked uncertainly.

"Why don't you go with Max? One of you can take each side of the street. Just tell them Harry Ostrom. Everybody knows him."

But nobody had seen him. On a Sunday afternoon, people were eating big dinners, taking naps, and watching television, or were over on the athletic field at the school, tossing or kicking balls.

When Buddy and Max met in the middle of the street at the intersection with the main highway, Max was scowling. "How far could he go, for pete's sake? In a town the size of this one, nobody can get really *lost,* can they? I mean, he might not be able to see to find his way home, but we ought to be able to find *him.*"

"Maybe Addie or Cassie has found him,"

Buddy said hopefully. "Let's go back to the house. Unless you think he might have crossed the highway. Should we ask over there on the other side?"

Max considered. "No. Not without checking at home. Just in case he's turned up."

But Grandpa had *not* turned up. Cassie was on the edge of tears. "Maybe we'd better call the police in to help look for him."

The police force in Haysville consisted of two officers and one patrol car. Both officers knew Grandpa, and even the one off-duty brought out his own car to help look.

By seven o'clock, when Buddy's stomach was starting to rumble, the entire town had been alerted, and remained baffled. Grandpa Harry Ostrom might have vanished into thin air.

By that time the temperature had dropped, and the darkened sky was overcast. A light rain had begun. Grandpa had been right about the weather changes that set off his arthritis.

"He'll get pneumonia if he's out in this," Cassie said, twisting her hands together.

"Buddy, look into his room and see if he took his blue sweater. And look on the hooks by the back door, near where we hang the keys. He has a dark blue jacket. See if it's there."

Both the sweater and the jacket were gone. Buddy stood for a minute in the middle of Grandpa's room, surveying his collection of books, magazines, miniatures of old cars, and bundles and packets, some of them spilling out of their wrappings.

The aunts, she knew, had tried to get him to get rid of some of it. She could see why. It would be impossible to clean, even if he'd allow them past the door. Yet she understood Grandpa's side of it, too.

Here in this room was the entire sum of Grandpa's life. His pictures, his treasures, and his memories had all been condensed into what would fit in this one room. Just as most of what remained in Buddy's life, except for Bart and Dad, was packed into that garage in the house she'd had to move out of. She hoped that she still would have Dad, when Bart came to get her, but it was easy to imagine how Grandpa felt about what he had left.

He could no longer see these things clearly. Most he would never use again. Yet they had been important to him, for one reason or another, and like his speaking clock, they helped keep him oriented. Except that now, she feared, he was disoriented, lost somewhere, perhaps even sick or hurt. Like Max, she didn't see how he could have completely disappeared in such a small community, where he was known to everyone. She was afraid for him.

She said a little prayer for his safety, and returned

to where the others were discussing options, to report, "He took both the sweater and the jacket."

"Thank the Lord for that," Cassie said, distress evident on her round face. "I hope we find him before he starves, or something worse."

"He ate enough for two men at dinner," Addie said dryly, "so it would take a few days for him to starve. And if he had another stroke or something, he'll be found sooner or later. He couldn't have gone far."

"But he might die of a stroke if he doesn't get medical help," Cassie said.

"He's nearly ninety-two years old. He's expressed a wish to go on to Heaven rather than get any older," Addie told her sister. "But don't put him in his grave yet. Chances are he sat down to rest or talk to someone. We'll find him."

Cassie's lips trembled. "But it's dark out, and cold. And it's starting to rain."

One of the police officers stopped by the house to report that they hadn't found Grandpa, but that they'd keep looking. Some of the neighbors had organized a group to go from house to house over the entire town. Addie and Cassie donned raincoats and hoods, for the rain was falling now in earnest, accompanied by rising winds, and set forth once more. "There's no sense in you two getting wet," Addie told Buddy and Max. "Gus has gone over to the Hayloft, so answer the phone if it rings. If anyone has any news, call the police and they'll find us and let us know."

The moment they walked out the door, Max said sourly, "He can't go hunt for Grandpa, but he can go sit with his buddies in the tavern." He made a rude noise.

Nobody had mentioned supper, but once the others had gone, Buddy asked, "Do you think it would be all right if we had something to eat?"

"Yeah, I'm hungry, too. I hope Grandpa isn't cold and tired and hungry and can't remember how to get home. But it won't help him if we're hungry, too. Come on. I think there was plenty of chicken left over, and cold biscuits, too."

Nobody called. Nobody came home. They tried to watch TV, but gave it up as a bad job since neither of them could follow a plot. Even the jokes on the sitcom reruns didn't seem funny.

Ten o'clock came, and they should have gone to bed, but neither of them could bring themselves to do it. At five minutes after, they heard the car drive into the side yard, and then the sound of the back door opening.

Both of them were on their feet, moving in that direction, before the aunts could get all the way into the house.

They were alone.

"You didn't find him yet?" Buddy cried, disbelieving.

"No. No sign of him, though Mrs. Eldridge thinks she may have seen him, a man in a dark blue jacket and a baseball cap," Addie said, shedding her raincoat and letting it drip on the floor as she hung it on one of the hooks. "But that was hours ago."

"Where did she see him?" Max asked. Buddy could tell he was just as distressed as she was.

"Over by the Hayloft," Cassie said, sounding very tired. "Of course he wasn't going there. We knew that, but we asked, anyway, just in case. He might have gotten confused and gone looking for Gus, who wasn't there then."

Gus had cut the old man off at the dinner table, Buddy remembered, when he'd tried to talk about the sermon. Had he thought to chase Gus down and insist on relating the whole thing? Of course Gus had still been home, upstairs taking a nap, when Grandpa left the house. But Grandpa might not have realized that.

Buddy's throat ached. "What are we going to do, then? Just . . . go to bed, and not look anymore until morning?" The thought of Grandpa wandering around out there in the dark and the wet made her want to cry. What if it was already too late to rescue him?

What if it was already too late to rescue Dad?

Her eyes brimmed, and the ache went down into her throat.

Beside her, Max suddenly exclaimed, "The keys!"

He said it so loudly that Buddy jumped.

"What keys?" Addie asked.

"His keys. The keys to the store. Remember, there was a set that never got turned over to Alf— the spares he kept for emergencies. They used to hang next to the jackets."

Buddy followed their collective gazes to the little hooks beside the dripping raincoats.

"He took them," Cassie breathed. "Oh, good grief, do you suppose that's where he went? Back to the store? He hasn't been there since Alf Peterson went bankrupt and they boarded it up."

Addie was already reaching for her soaked coat to put it back on. "The way his memory is, he might think he was there yesterday. Let's go look! Get a couple of flashlights. The power's been turned off there for ages."

"We're coming, too," Max asserted, and when nobody argued, he grabbed his own jacket and thrust another one at Buddy. "Come on!"

The jacket was much too big, but it had a hood, and Buddy wrapped up in it and hurried with the others back out to the detached garage. She piled into the backseat with Max, and Addie started up the car and backed it out to the street.

Buddy remembered the closed store on the main street that was also the state highway. Ostrom

Appliances, the store Grandpa had operated for most of his adult life. Alf Peterson hadn't bothered to change the name when he'd bought it.

There was no one on the street at this time of night. They passed the Hayloft, the only building with neon lights still burning, sending vivid colors reflecting off the wet pavement. A few cars were parked in front and beside it, but the curb was empty in front of the old store building.

Addie cut the engine, and they all bailed out. "He took the only key we have, so I hope if he's here he left the front door unlocked," she said, and rattled the knob on one of the double doors.

It opened under her hand, and she switched on the big flashlight she carried. "Grandpa? Are you in here?"

There was no response.

Max carried a light, too, and swung it around the big main room, empty except for a long counter and some shelves behind it. The place had an unpleasant, musty smell, like mice.

"Grandpa!" Cassie shouted. "Where are you?"

And then they heard it, the mechanical little voice. "The time is 10:37 P.M."

"In the office," Addie said, and they all moved together, the twin globes of light making sweeping motions through the dust and cobwebs.

Grandpa was sitting on the floor beside an old-fashioned woodstove, hunched over with his arms

144

around his drawn-up knees. He blinked in their lights before they lowered them. "It's cold," he said. "I couldn't find anything to make a fire with. I always used to keep something to build a fire. Somebody's used it all up."

"Thank God you're all right," Cassie said, her voice breaking. "Come on, let us help you up. Can you stand?"

She and Max together got him on his feet, steering him toward the entrance at the front of the building.

"Why didn't anybody leave any kindling?" Grandpa asked. "Somebody's robbed the place. There's not a thing left here. We have to call the police."

"We will," Cassie said, "as soon as we get you home."

But Addie said, "It's not your store anymore, Grandpa. They moved everything out of it a long time ago. What did you do with the keys? I need to lock the door behind us."

Grandpa produced the keys, and his hands shook. "It's too cold," he said.

They went out into the night, and the old man was bundled into the backseat, between Buddy and Max. He was trembling, and Buddy could feel how frail and weak he was against her side.

*Thank you, God,* she whispered. *We found him in time.* Now if Bart could just find Dad, too.

Cassie insisted that Grandpa get into a hot bath while she got pajamas and a robe for him. "He's half-frozen," she said. "You kids, heat some soup for him, will you? Addie, will you call the police and tell them we found him?"

It wasn't until the old man had been warmed and fed and hustled off to bed that Addie exploded. She wasn't loud, but she was upset and very determined. "Cassie, this has got to stop. We can't keep trying to cope with this dementia by ourselves any longer. He's dangerous to himself, and he's dangerous to us."

Cassie's chin quivered as she stared her sister in the face. "He's our grandfather. We're living in his house. We're going to take care of him as long as he lives, the way we promised Mama and Grandma that we would."

"Of course we'll see that he's *taken care of*. But not by ourselves. He needs to be where he can't wander away, can't attempt to use the stove or the microwave, can't do anything dangerous. We can't watch him every minute here, Cassie. He needs to be in a rest home with professional caretakers who can keep track of him around the clock."

Cassie's eyes filled with moisture as she spoke with equal firmness. "But there's no such place here in Haysville. If we put him in one of those rest homes, he'd be away from everybody he knows.

Even we couldn't see him every day, and if we only visited him once or twice a week, he wouldn't remember from one time to the next. He'd think he'd been abandoned. He wouldn't meet friends at church; people couldn't drop in and see him at home the way they do here."

"We're not going through another day like this one," Addie said flatly. "I'm going to talk to Dr. Grant on Monday and see what he recommends. If I have to, I'll get Gordon up here to cast his vote with mine. But you've got to understand that we can't keep him at home any longer. It's not safe. Not for him, and not for us."

Tears leaked onto Cassie's cheeks. "I'll sleep down here. I'll watch him more closely, even at night."

"You're only one person, Cassie. And you have to sleep sometime. Speaking of sleep, you two kids get to bed. You've got school in the morning."

Behind them, as Buddy and Max headed for the sewing room and the stairs, they heard Cassie's tearful voice, pleading, and Addie's determined one.

Buddy blinked back her own tears as she closed the door behind her and put on her pajamas. Nobody had reminded her to wash her face or brush her teeth, so she decided to skip it until morning. She prayed for Bart, and Dad, and Grandpa, and for herself. She didn't want to go to school in this unfamiliar town. She didn't want to cry, and get her head all plugged up so that she got a headache, but she couldn't help it.

She turned out the light and hugged her pillow—the strange, too-thin pillow that didn't feel anything like the one she'd left behind—wondering if she'd ever go to sleep happy again.

# 12

Buddy had changed schools before, a number of times, but never had she dreaded it as much as she did this time.

It had done no good to protest that surely her brother and her father would be coming soon to pick her up, that it was pointless to enroll in a new school for just a few days. It hadn't helped to remind Cassie that no one had gotten to bed until late last night, and that what sleep they'd had hadn't been restful.

It didn't even matter that Grandpa had again been cause for concern at breakfast, when he was despondent and confused and uncooperative. He hadn't wanted to get out of bed, he wanted to know why he wasn't in his old room upstairs, and he insisted that he did not like scrambled eggs, even with sausage.

"But they've always been your favorite!" Cassie exclaimed, sounding mildly provoked. "I made them special for you today!"

The old man's mouth took on a mutinous pout. "Don't you think I know what I like?" Grandpa demanded, making Cassie roll her eyes. "I don't like scrambled eggs!"

Addie pushed back her own chair. "Well, you two work it out. Let him have cold cereal for once, if that's what he wants. It won't hurt him. Max, you and Buddy better get going. See that she gets to the right classroom and finds her way around. I need to get to work upstairs; I have a chapter almost finished."

Now it was Max's turn to roll his eyes, and though she was quite apprehensive herself, Buddy took pity on him. "You don't have to take me around like I'm a baby," she said. "I know where the office is, and they'll tell me where to go, won't they?"

"You'll get Mrs. Hope." Max made a derisive snorting noise. "Wrong name. They should call her Mrs. Pity-Party."

Immediately tense, Buddy asked, "Why? What's wrong with her?"

"She likes nothing better than to find out what's wrong with everybody, and then make a big public display of it. If you go in with a cast on your arm, she has to know how you broke it, and all the particulars, then tell all the details to the whole class. When she had her gallbladder out we got to know all about it, including how she threw up from the anesthetic. I was surprised she didn't show us the scar. So if I were you, I'd keep quiet about how your dad disappeared. She'll make a federal case of it, for sure. She probably already knows about Pa falling down and getting a concussion. I guess everybody in Hayseed knows." He sounded glum.

Buddy decided her stomach was too uneasy to finish her breakfast. "Hayseed? Is that what you call Haysville?"

"It's a hayseed town. Nothing happens here. No movies, no bowling alley, a library that's only open two days a week. Everybody knows everybody else's business, and they tell. Don't be surprised if people ask you about Pa, and Grandpa, and all your own business that's none of theirs."

For a few more minutes Buddy lingered, hoping against hope that Bart would call with good news and make going to school today unnecessary.

But the phone was stubbornly silent. Talking clock going off every few minutes, Grandpa retreated to his bedroom, refusing Cassie permission to come and straighten it up. There was nothing to do but leave.

Buddy had expected that Max would not even want to be seen walking to school with her, but he fell into step beside her. Obviously he had decided the smell would be gone from his room, or if it wasn't, the class would have to use it, anyway.

"I've been a Hayseed all my life," Max said. "My mom liked it here when she first came, she said. She liked a small, friendly town. Until Pa took to drinking too much, and everybody in town knew about it. Nobody actually came out and said anything to *her* about him, but she said she always knew they were thinking about it. It was humiliating and embarrassing."

"Where is she now?" Buddy asked, grateful that she wasn't making this walk alone. She saw other kids heading toward the school, too, and some of them glanced at her curiously, but none of them spoke except a couple of boys who greeted Max.

"Last two letters came from Fort Worth. Texas, you know. She said she had a good job there, and had met an interesting man. They were just friends, but she liked him a lot. She sent me money for some new jeans and a shirt. She said she'd have sent more but she wanted to save enough so maybe by next summer she can get me a bus ticket and I can go see her. I was never in Texas, but I've read about it a lot. I hope I get to go."

"I hope you do, too," Buddy said sincerely. She wondered where she would be next summer, or even if she might still be stuck here in Hayseed. It seemed a more appropriate name than Haysville.

That morning there were kids in the office at

the school, along with Mr. Faulkner and Sylvia. The secretary was speaking sharply to a tall, unkempt-looking girl dragging a battered backpack on the floor.

"I've told you before, Myra, you can't come to school smelling like horse liniment and the barnyard. The other kids refuse to sit next to you."

"I can't help it," Myra whined. "My ma makes me."

"Then tell your mother I want to talk to her. You'll have to take a bath before you come to school."

"There's no hot water. The heater's broke, and we can't get a new one until Dad gets paid next week. I'm not taking a bath in cold water, even if I have to stay home from school," Myra said defiantly.

"You have a kitchen stove, don't you? Put some water in a pan, heat it on the stove, and take a sponge bath. And use soap, or that smell won't come off." Sylvia glanced past the unhappy student and saw Buddy. "Oh, good morning, Amy Kate. I'll be with you in just a minute. Now, Myra, you can ask Mrs. Murphy if she wants you to stay and sit in the back away from everyone else, or go home and scrub up before you come back. Dust yourself with baby powder afterward; that might help."

Myra turned sullenly away from the desk, and Buddy felt a moment of compassion for her. The girl might not be homeless, living in a car, but she certainly had problems.

"Now," Sylvia said, smiling, "let's see who we can find to take you to your room." She glanced around the office at the milling kids, most of them looking unhappy. "Sara Jenks, you're in Mrs. Hope's homeroom. Will you take Amy Kate back with you, please, and introduce her?"

Sara was a small, thin girl with very thick glasses. "I need a pass to leave school at eleven o'clock," she said, giving Buddy only a cursory glance. "Mom's got a doctor's appointment in Kalispell this afternoon, and I have to go along and baby-sit Junior."

Sylvia's smile congealed. "I told your mother she can't keep taking you out of school to baby-sit, Sara."

The girl shrugged. "You want me to bring him to school with me? He's only eight months old, and we can't leave him home alone. I gotta go unless I can keep him with me here, and Mrs. Hope didn't like it the last time. Everybody wanted to play with him and didn't pay any attention to her."

Sylvia appeared to grind her teeth. "Well, I'll give you the pass this time, but you tell your mother I need to talk to her about this. She'll have to make other arrangements for the baby next time." She scribbled out a pink pass and handed it over. "Now, show Amy Kate where to go, all right?"

The girl said nothing to Buddy, who simply followed her out of the office. The hallway was full of noisy kids, laughing, yelling, and shoving. Sara led the way up the stairs, turning to the right at the top. She didn't speak until they'd reached the door of a room with a sign on it that said, MRS. HOPE.

"You the one who's been abandoned?" she asked then.

Buddy's heart was jolted. "No! My dad went away to take a new job, and something happened to him, but my brother's looking for him. I'm only staying with my aunts until they come get me."

Sara nodded. "Everybody talks in this town, but they never get anything right. If they tell you my mom's got cancer, it's not so. She's getting treatment for a disease with a big, long name, but it's not cancer. She's going to get better."

"I'm glad," Buddy said, and she was. "My mom died in a car wreck."

Sara opened the door to Mrs. Hope's room and moved toward the teacher's desk. She laid the pink slip in front of the middle-aged lady and said, "This is Amy Kate, but they call her Buddy."

Buddy certainly hadn't told her that. Her ears felt hot, knowing that people were talking about her, and they were saying things that weren't true.

Her dad never would have abandoned her and Bart.

"Hello, Buddy," Mrs. Hope said.

Several kids snickered, and one boy even asked under his breath, "What kind of name is that for a girl?" Buddy felt the heat creep up her neck, flooding her face.

Mrs. Hope was scowling at the pink slip. "Again? Sara, how do you expect to keep up your grades if you keep missing school?"

Buddy didn't listen to their conversation. She was acutely aware of the other kids, already in their seats, watching her. Two girls sitting next to each other leaned toward the middle of the aisle, putting their hands over their mouths as they whispered and laughed.

At what, she wondered? Her name? Her red face? Her haircut, or her clothes?

What if Bart and Dad didn't come for her soon? She'd have to stay here, going to this school, with these kids whose eyes appraised her hair and her clothes and everything about her. They probably all believed that she'd been abandoned. The heat spread from her ears to her cheeks, and she was helpless to control it.

"Class," Mrs. Hope announced, "this is Amy Kate, but she likes to be called Buddy."

Buddy wanted to speak out and deny that, to tell them to call her by her real name, but her tongue seemed to be stuck to the roof of her mouth. She couldn't make a sound.

"Maybe she'll tell us, when we get better acquainted, how she came by that nickname. There's an empty seat in the second row, there, beside Elinor. Just take that desk."

Buddy slid into the designated seat, which felt strange, as if it didn't fit her. She resented having to be here, when she was only going to be in town for a few more days. Surely she'd hear from Bart soon, and she'd have gone through all of this for nothing.

Dad had said that if this job worked out, they might be moving, and then she and Bart would both have to enroll in new schools, but that would be different. They'd be in a town where they were going to stay, where she'd have time to make friends.

None of these kids looked like friends. They were examining her as if she were a new variety of beetle in a glass jar.

The girl across the aisle—Elinor?—asked abruptly, "Who cut your hair?"

Immediately Buddy stiffened defensively. Did that mean the girl thought it was awful, or did she like it?" She swallowed. "My aunt," she admitted.

"Hmm. I thought maybe it was one of those fancy stylists, like the models have. It makes you look kind of . . . exotic."

Exotic? That was good, wasn't it? Tentatively, relaxing a little, Buddy smiled, and Elinor smiled back.

That was the only friendly overture, though. The teacher was kindly, but clearly too busy to spend much time on a new student. Not that Buddy wanted her attention. She remembered what Max had said about the way Mrs. Hope knew everything about everybody and didn't hesitate to talk about it.

It was nearing the noon hour when an older student opened the door to the classroom. She conveyed a note to the front of the room, and Mrs. Hope paused in her explanation of a difficult math problem to read it, then looked directly at Buddy. "Amy Kate," she said, not using the nickname this time, "you're to go to the office immediately."

Of course Buddy hadn't done anything wrong. She couldn't have. But her heart raced as if she were guilty of *something*.

Awkwardly, Buddy stood up and moved toward the door. Once more everyone in the room was staring at her. The student messenger handed her one of the pink slips that gave permission to leave the classroom, and Buddy followed her out into the hallway. "Is something wrong?" she asked the older girl.

"I think your aunt is here to get you. I don't know why," the girl said.

Buddy didn't know whether to be excited or apprehensive. Was it about Dad, and Bart? Or had something happened to Grandpa?

Addie was standing in the lower hallway at the door to the office. She didn't waste any time. "Your brother's waiting for you to call him back," she said. "He's found Dan."

# 13

Buddy's fingers trembled as she dialed the number Cassie had written down. She could hardly breathe waiting for Bart to pick up at the other end.

"Buddy?" her brother's voice asked over the line.

"Yes! Is Dad okay?"

"Well, he's alive. Maybe not okay." Buddy's heart did a flip-flop, and she missed a few words. "He's in a hospital now, and the doctors are still evaluating him. I didn't want to wait until they finish that before I told you. It's an incredible story—I won't try to tell it all over the phone. He was conscious, though, when we found him. He knew who I was, and asked about you."

Buddy had to sit down because her legs refused

to hold her up. Cassie and Addie and Grandpa were all standing around, staring at her.

"Dad's hurt, he's in a hospital," she told them, eyes suddenly brimming.

"Oh, Buddy," Cassie said, putting a hand on her arm.

Addie didn't say anything, but her knuckles were white where she gripped the back of another chair, waiting.

"Listen, I'm going to get something to eat," Bart was saying in her ear. "As soon as I get a full report, I'll call you back. I'll probably come get you and bring you here, because Dad's going to be stuck here for a few days, anyway. Okay?"

"Okay!" Buddy agreed tremulously. "I'll be right here when you call back. Can't you just tell me what happened to him?"

"He and Rich went over a cliff along Highway 101, and nobody was even looking for them there until I came along. The trucking company apparently was convinced they'd hijacked the load and peddled it somewhere, then hidden the rig back in one of those canyons where nobody'd find it for a long time. Rich is here in the hospital, too, with a broken leg and a dislocated shoulder. I called his mom. Somebody wants to use this phone, and I don't know any more, anyway. I'll call you back, Buddy."

A click severed the connection, and she was

unable to keep the tears from running down her face as she looked at her aunts and Grandpa. "He went over a cliff. The man with him was hurt, too. Bart's going to call back as soon as the doctors can tell him anything," she said. "But they're both alive, even if they're hurt."

"Praise the Lord," Grandpa said. For once, his mind seemed perfectly clear. "I never believed that Dan would abandon his children. He was the best salesman I ever had. He never shirked his responsibilities. I like that in a man." He looked suddenly at Addie. "You held it against him, Sister, that he married your little sister instead of you. But he never promised to marry you, did he, girl?"

Addie loosened her grip on the table. "No, he didn't." Her face flamed bright pink, then faded out until she was very pale. "But we were good friends. He *would* have asked me if EllaBelle hadn't come home from college and stolen him away from me. Everybody in town expected us to get married. Pastor even asked me when we were going to set the date."

Now twin spots of pink appeared in her cheeks. "It was so humiliating. Dan and I had run around together that whole winter, after he went to work for you in the store. We liked all the same things, read the same books, enjoyed the same music. I knew he was going to propose to me.

And then *she* came home, and he couldn't see anybody but her."

"She was so lively, wasn't she?" Grandpa observed, not seeming to notice Addie's pain. Still so strong, it was, after all these years, Buddy thought. But how could Mama have stolen Dad; he who hadn't really belonged to Addie. "Always laughing, I remember. Looked a lot like little missy here. What's your name again, child?"

"She's Buddy, Grandpa," Cassie reminded him.

Grandpa frowned. "Silly name for a pretty little girl," he said.

Buddy cleared her throat and swiped at her eyes. "It's really Amy Kate, but when I was only about three, Daddy used to call me his little buddy when I went with him in the truck, and then everybody started calling me that."

Grandpa's fingers touched the talking clock, and it announced the time. "Have we had lunch yet? I seem to be hungry."

"No, we haven't, but I'll fix it right now," Cassie assured him. "Somebody's at the door, probably the mailman. Would you get it, Buddy? I'll start dishing up the soup, and I was going to make toasted cheese sandwiches."

Buddy felt shaky as she obediently headed for the door. Surely they wouldn't make her go back to school now, would they? Even after Bart called back to tell her how seriously injured Dad was? If her brother was coming to get her in only a few days, there couldn't be any compelling reason to return to school.

It was, indeed, the mailman. He extended a handful of letters, and then dug into his pouch for a rather battered manila envelope. "Sorry about this one. Got damaged in the mail, somehow. Came open, looks like. They stuck everything back into it, I guess, but she'll probably have to run off another copy of it if she sends it out again. Some of the pages are dirty, like they got walked on. Good thing she's got one of those printer things."

Buddy thanked him and accepted it, only to have it fall apart again, scattering pages all over the hall floor. She set the rest of the mail aside, noticing that the one on top was addressed to Max. His mother, maybe? She got down on her knees to pick up the loose pages and heard Addie come up behind her.

"What on earth's going on?" Addie asked. "Is that one of my manuscripts?"

"Yes. It broke open," Buddy said, wondering if she should try to sort them out by page numbers or just gather them in a stack for Addie to straighten out. She picked up the next page and hesitated. "This seems to be a letter, not part of the book," she said, and handed it up to Addie.

Her aunt glanced at the sheet of paper, then for

the second time in only a few minutes got white enough that Buddy wondered if she was going to faint. When Addie made a sort of gurgling sound, Buddy stood up quickly and grabbed Addie's arm, guiding her toward the chair at the telephone table. "Are you all right?" Buddy asked, putting the rest of the mail down. "Shall I get Aunt Cassie?"

Addie's lips moved, but she didn't make any sound at first. Then she thrust the letter into Buddy's hand.

Buddy read it aloud. "'Dear Miss Ostrom: We are pleased to accept your historical novel, *Winds of Change,* and to offer you the enclosed contract for an advance of . . .'" Buddy's voice trailed off in a little squeak.

"Does it say *ten thousand dollars?*" Addie whispered, brushing her fingertips across her lips.

Buddy wondered as if her own lips were pale, too. "Yes. Ten thousand dollars."

Addie appeared to collapse inwardly, as she were a tire going flat. "What does the rest of it say?"

Buddy read it silently this time, feeling almost as stunned as Addie looked, then summarized. "They want you to do some revisions. It says they think Rosemary sounds too mature for a six-year-old. . . . Rosemary's one of the characters?"

"I based her on . . . EllaBelle, when she was

six," Addie breathed. "She talked ... just like that. Grandpa said she was ... a little dictionary."

"Addie? Buddy? What are you doing?"

Cassie sounded cross. "I thought you two would come and at least set the table while I tended the toasted cheese. . . . Why is the mail all over the floor?"

Buddy moistened her lips when it appeared that Addie was too stricken to explain.

"Aunt Addie's just sold one of her books. They want her to make a few changes, something about a little girl who seems too mature for her age."

Cassie's mouth formed an incredulous O. She, too, needed to sit down, but there was only one chair in the hallway, so she leaned against the wall and clutched at her throat.

Buddy wasn't sure what else to say. She looked at the pages scattered on the floor. "Somebody walked on some of them. They'll have to be done over, won't they?"

Addie was gathering her wits and her breath. "I'll run off another copy, after I've done whatever revisions they're asking for."

"Are they paying you for this book?" Cassie asked, color returning to her face.

"Yes, of course," Addie said, sounding a bit short-tempered. "How could I sell it if they didn't pay for it?"

On her knees, trying to sort through the pages,

Buddy heard footsteps behind Cassie and looked up to see Gus standing there. His mouth was sagging open.

Addie noticed him and smiled a brittle smile. "You were wrong, Gus. I wasn't wasting my time after all. I was practicing a craft, learning it, getting better at it, and it's finally paying off. They're buying my book."

"For enough to pay the bills?" Cassie asked breathlessly. "So you can replace the microwave? And the remote control?"

Addie pulled herself together and stood up. "Yes, enough to replace them both. Pick up the whole mess, Buddy, and put it on the dining room table. I'll sort the pages after lunch. I'll take the rest of the mail."

"Lunch!" Cassie shrieked, and fled toward the kitchen.

"I turned over the sandwiches," they heard Grandpa say from the doorway. "That one got a little burned, but I like it that way. I'll take that one."

Between hearing that Dan had been found alive, even though injured, and that Addie had at long last sold a book for a substantial amount of money, it was doubtful that any of them were aware of whether their sandwiches were scorched or not.

And when the phone rang an hour later,

everyone took it for granted that it was Bart calling back. Buddy raced for it.

"Buddy? The doctors said Dad's dehydrated, and he's got a nasty gash on his head that's infected, but they're giving him antibiotics and fluids in IVs. He broke a couple of ribs and some bones in his left hand, but otherwise it's practically a miracle. The cops said they'd have expected anybody who went off that cliff to have been killed, so it really *is* miraculous."

Buddy remembered her prayers in the long nights since they'd heard from Dad. Her throat ached as she asked, "How long will he have to be in the hospital? Where are you, anyway?"

"At Willits, in northern California. They think probably only a few days, but I don't want to wait until I can take him home before I come get you. I mean, we don't even have a home now, do we? So I don't know where we'll go, actually, but Dad'll probably help us decide that after he's had something to eat and some rest. He said he kept thinking about those steaks we were going to have when he got home, but for right now the nurse said he'll probably get hot soup and crackers."

"How come it took so long to find him?" Buddy wanted to know. "How come nobody noticed he'd been in a wreck?"

Bart sounded so close, she could have reached out and touched him, and she wished she could, and Dad, too. "The truck was swept through the railing and down the side of the mountain by a gigantic mud slide. Remember, it had been raining for days? A chunk of the mountain above the road came down, and just swept everything over the edge. It carried the truck and Dad and Rich along with it, and practically buried them. They went down almost four hundred feet, and nobody could see the wreckage from the road up over their heads."

Buddy shuddered, imagining how close they'd come to losing their father. "How did you find him, then?"

"Well, I was asking at every place I came to, all along that stretch of road. Several people—a waitress, and a guy at a fuel stop—remembered seeing the truck and Dad and Rich. So I knew they'd gone a certain distance. I saw there had been trouble with the road—it's still only one lane along that stretch because they have to rebuild a section of it—and when I couldn't run down any trace of them beyond that point, I talked to the local sheriff's department and then to the trucking company in Lewiston again. I knew they couldn't have stolen a load of lumber or anything else; there was no place they could have gone in that area. Nobody had even thought of looking through all the debris at the bottom of the cliff. There were rocks in it, big as cars, and trees, tumbled every which way, all over the top of the mud. Their CB didn't work down there, couldn't get out to reach anybody so far above them. There's a river at the bottom of the canyon, but no roads into that area. The search and rescue people came, and some of them went down on ropes because the canyon was too narrow to check it out with a helicopter. I was standing there on what's left of the highway when they signaled that they'd found the truck, and for a few minutes none of us up there knew whether Dad had survived the wreck or not. Then some more guys went down on ropes, and they got shovels and stuff to dig them out, and brought Dad and Rich up on those metal mesh stretchers."

Buddy shuddered, imagining what it must have been like to stand there, watching and wondering if Dad was still alive or if he'd died in the wreck, maybe even suffocated in the mud that covered his rig. "It must have been horrible," she murmured.

"Well, it was some relief when they let us know both Dad and Rich were alive. But they looked awful when they came up over the edge of the canyon. I mean, besides being really dirty and bloody because they had cuts and scratches, Dad looked half-starved. He said Rich had had a couple of candy bars in a jacket pocket, and Dad had some peanuts. That's all they'd had to eat the whole time. And they'd each had a Thermos of coffee. After that ran out, they didn't have anything to drink. And of course they'd both been several days without shaving, so they looked pretty grim. But Dad knew I was there, and he reached out and squeezed my hand and said my name. And he asked about you."

So much for all those people who'd insisted he must have abandoned them, Buddy thought, tearing up again. She'd *known* he'd never have done any such thing. "And he's going to be all right, isn't he? He's going to heal back to normal?" she asked.

"They're pretty sure he is. Only it'll take a while."

Buddy licked her lips, glancing up at the audience that had gathered around her—both aunts and Grandpa. "What will we do until he's better?"

"I haven't figured that out yet. But don't worry," Bart told her. "At least we'll all be together again."

Cassie made a sound, deep in her throat. "He's hurt, right? He's going to need some time to recuperate. And you don't have a house anymore."

Addie moved, just a little, as if to stop Cassie from making an offer, but she didn't say anything.

"He could come here," Cassie said. "Bart could bring him here."

This time, Addie spoke. "Where are you going

to put them? Two more people? Cassie, we don't have the space."

"Are you still holding a grudge against him for marrying EllaBelle?" Cassie challenged her. "You could move your desk and computer into your bedroom for a few weeks, couldn't you? We could set up a bed in the back bedroom for Dan; there's still the bed that was in there years ago. And there are twin beds in Max's room. He wouldn't mind sharing with Bart for a while."

Addie's face had flamed bright pink. "I'm not holding a grudge because he married Ellie! For pete's sake, Cassie!"

"Well, then, Buddy, tell them to come here until he's well enough to go back to work. That way you and Bart could go to school and not get behind."

Buddy didn't want to go back to school. She'd hoped when Addie came to take her home that she would never have to walk back into Mrs. Hope's classroom with all those strange kids looking at her. But a man just out of the hospital, with very little money, couldn't live in a car.

On the phone, Bart was demanding, "What's going on? What are they saying?"

"Let me talk to him," Cassie said, and took the receiver out of Buddy's hand and began to lay out her idea for him. When she finished, she smiled and handed it back to Buddy. "He thinks that would probably work," she said. "Better than coming here and taking you away when you don't have a place to live. If it's only going to be a few days before Dan's released from the hospital, it would make more sense for them both to come here. He's going to talk to Dan and see what he says."

Dad would probably say, "Yes, thank you," Buddy thought. And maybe it would be easier than anything else they could do right away. "What do you think?" she asked her brother, and heard relief in Bart's voice.

"It sounds better than holing up in a motel, when we're short of money already," he said. "He'll have comp payments until he can work again, but I guess they aren't very much. I'll talk to Dad and call you back, okay?"

"Where are you sleeping now?" Buddy demanded. "Not still in the car, I hope."

"No, they're letting me take the other bed in Dad's room. Hang in there, Buddy, till I get back to you."

She felt very shaky as she hung up the phone. "He's going to talk to Dad," she said, addressing Cassie.

"Good. Dan's smart enough to do the sensible thing, which is to stay here. He's not going to call back right away, now, so you might as well go back to school, honey."

"No," Buddy protested. "It's almost time for school to get out, and I'd just disrupt the class going back in now."

Unexpectedly Addie came to her aid. "She's right. What difference does one afternoon make? She can come upstairs and help me start clearing out that back bedroom so we can set up the bed in there again."

"Can I have my old room back?" Grandpa asked. "I always liked my old room."

"No, dear," Cassie said. "Gus and I are in that room now. And you had trouble on the stairs, remember? We don't want you to fall down the stairs again."

Grandpa scowled. "Did I fall down the stairs?"

"Yes. Twice," Cassie told him. "Go along, then, Buddy, and help Addie. This will all work out just fine. Did they say when they'd pay you for the book, Addie? How long it would be before you have the money?"

"No. Not until after I've made the revisions they asked for, I suppose," Addie said. "I'm still in shock. I don't quite believe it yet, that it's finally happened. I always thought it would happen eventually, though, even if Gus thought I was wasting my time."

"You always told good stories, Addie," Cassie said. "I prayed that you'd sell one sometime."

"I'll sell more than one," Addie said, her good

spirits returning. "This is the sixth publisher who's seen this book, and they liked it. Maybe they'll like some of the other ones I've got stuck in a drawer upstairs. They haven't seen my newest one that just came back from another publisher. Come on, Buddy, let's go see what we can do to make room for two more people."

Buddy trailed her up the stairs, torn between joy over her father's rescue and despair over being stuck in school there for a few more weeks, or even months.

She remembered, somewhat belatedly, to say a silent *Thank you, God* as she followed Addie into the room that had served her as an office. Now if she could just figure out what had happened to the money that Addie thought her mother had stolen, everything would be all right. At least much better, she amended, thinking of Grandpa and the problems he had. Much, much better for her and Bart and Dad, anyway.

She couldn't bear to have anyone think that her mother had been a thief. She was certain it wasn't true, but she didn't know any way to prove it.

# 14

"What's going on?" Max demanded, sticking his head through the doorway to where Addie and Buddy were wrestling to set up an old-fashioned brass bed in the back bedroom where Addie's desk had been.

"Bart found my dad," Buddy told him, beaming. "He's going to come here to recuperate when he gets out of the hospital."

"No kidding! What happened to him?"

For once the story hadn't gotten all over town within ten minutes. Buddy happily related as much as she knew while Addie went off to get sheets and blankets.

"That's great," Max said. He was carrying the kitten, which purred loudly against his chest as he stroked him. "I heard you went home from school, but nobody knew why."

"Did you get the letter that came today? Was it from your mom?"

"I didn't see it. It wasn't with the mail downstairs. Maybe Addie picked it up," Max guessed. "Sometimes she sticks it in her pocket so my old man doesn't see it. He froths at the mouth when anybody mentions my mom. I don't know why. Sure, she left him, but he deserved it. And he's married to Cassie now, so why does he care about what my mom does?"

"Did you talk to Addie at all? Did she tell you *her* news?"

Max stopped petting the kitten. "No. What?"

Addie came to the doorway behind him, her arms full of linens. "I sold a book."

Max's eyes went wide. "A book? You sold one of 'em? Wow! Did they send you a check?"

"No. I have to do some revisions on it first, then sign the contract and send it back before they get to that. But they've offered me ten thousand dollars. That's not too bad for a *first* book, do you think? Well, of course it isn't my first book, it's just my first *sale*."

Max let out a triumphant yelp. "All right! I hope my old man turned green."

A small smile softened Addie's mouth. "Almost, I think. I reminded him of what he'd said about my wasting time."

"What did he say?" Max asked eagerly.

"Not much of anything. I think Gus was

speechless for once." Addie plunked the bedding down on a chair and picked out a fitted sheet. "Grab that corner, Buddy."

"Wish he'd stay that way," Max said. "But he probably won't. Did I get a letter from my mom?"

"Yes. I almost forgot about it." Addie pulled it out of her pocket and handed it over.

"Congratulations," Max said, taking the letter. "I hope you sell all the rest of them, too. Come on, Scamp, let's go read our letter."

Buddy was somewhat disappointed when Max retreated to his own room. She'd hoped he had good news, too, and that he'd share it.

Some of what she was feeling must have shown on her face, for Addie paused in the act of putting a flowered case on a pillow. "He always likes to read the letters from his mother in private. I suspect sometimes they make him cry, and he doesn't want anyone to see him."

"Oh," Buddy said. "I hope it's a nice letter. You have wonderful news today, and so do I. I want Max to have something good to think about, too."

"He doesn't have an easy time, with Gus for a father," Addie said, plumping the pillow and placing it on the bed, then reaching for the other one. "But he's a good kid. He'll be all right."

Silently, Buddy helped finish making up the bed for her father, including smoothing out the bedspread to go over it. Her own future was uncertain—how long would Dad be unable to work? Would he get this newest job back when he could drive again? And where would they go, back to Washington State or somewhere else? But at least Dad was alive, and he'd get back on his feet, and they'd be together somewhere as a family again.

"There," Addie said as they straightened up across the bed from each other. "I'm sorry we can't find somewhere else to put the rest of those boxes. There's not much room in the attic, and those stairs are enough to kill anybody. But at least he can rest comfortably. Now I need to arrange the stuff we moved out of here. Will you help me set up the computer and printer in my bedroom so I can work there? I want to do those revisions as soon as I can."

They walked down the hallway together to Addie's room. "You said you based a little girl character on my mother," Buddy said. "Why?"

"Why?" Addie echoed. "Well, because she was a charming little girl, and I wanted a character like that."

"So you liked her before she . . . ran off and married my dad."

"Of course I liked her," Addie said. She shoved the desk into a better position and lifted the computer monitor onto it. "Can you get down under the desk and plug this in? I guess I'll have to put the printer on the other side now. There's an outlet right in the middle under there, so I'll pass that cord down to you, too."

"But if you really liked her, how could you hate her now?" Buddy wanted to know.

Addie gave her an exasperated look. "I don't hate her. I'll admit I resented it when she showed up and made Dan forget all about me. I really thought he was going to marry me, and it was . . . very disappointing, when they just took off together. It was a big shock, and very humiliating. In a town the size of this one, everybody knew about it and felt sorry for me. It's uncomfortable to have people pitying you."

Buddy, down on her knees, plugged in the two electrical cords, then backed out of the kneehole on the desk. "They fell in love. I don't think either of them meant to hurt you, Aunt Addie."

"No, I don't suppose they did. But it did hurt." Addie lifted the power tower and set it beside the monitor, busy hooking up connections. "There, let's see if we've done it right so it works." She started pressing buttons, and the monitor lighted up for her to check her password. "Good. I'm ready to go to work."

Buddy stood up and hesitated, wanting to say more, afraid to do it. "I don't see how you can believe that Mama was a thief. That she stole Grandpa's money. She always taught Bart and me to be truthful, to be honest. Once, Bart swiped a candy bar in a store and she made him take it back and apologize. Why did you think she stole money from Grandpa?"

Addie stood very still. "Because she was the only one who could have taken it. I'm sorry, Buddy, but she was here the day the money was delivered to Grandpa. It was foolish, but he insisted on cash instead of a check because he didn't trust the man who was buying the store. Well, that part wasn't foolish—Alf Peterson really wasn't trustworthy—but we should have insisted on a cashier's check for the major share of the money and not let Grandpa dictate the terms. He had all that cash in a bag, a small case, and we expected to take it to the bank later in the day. Only when we went to get it, it was gone."

Buddy stared at her, incredulous. "But that's crazy! *Mama* couldn't have taken it! She never would have done something like that! If you knew her, how could you even think it?"

Addie was reacting as if to something very stressful. Her face had once more gone very pink, and now was so white that Buddy wondered if she was about to faint, but she stood there supporting herself with a hand on the edge of the desk.

"Obviously you don't understand what the situation was, Buddy. She knew that Dan and I had been seeing each other while she was away at college. Yet she blew in here in a swirl of curls and pretty skirts and swept him right out from under my nose, and they ran off and got married without even telling me. Up until then, I'd trusted her, but I was never able to trust her again."

"But that was years ago! I don't think she even knew you were in love with Dad; she never said anything except that you'd been friends. And if Dad had been in love with *you,* he never would have eloped with *her!* She never knew why you cut her off the way you did, didn't write to her or anything. She'd say, 'We used to be friends, when I was a kid,' but she couldn't have known, Aunt Addie!"

"She was your mother," Addie said, sounding cold. "So naturally you thought well of her. But EllaBelle was here on the day Grandpa got the money for the store, and she helped him pack it in that bag, and Herbert Faulkner saw the bag beside her on the seat as she was leaving town. He admitted that to me later, and while he's a little wimp of a school principal, I never had any reason to believe he was a liar. It was a distinctive bag, a flowered one, that had belonged to Cassie. She'd loaned it to him to carry the money, and Herbert saw it. He couldn't possibly have been mistaken in that."

Buddy felt as if someone had struck her in the chest, knocking all the wind out of her. "But someone must have been mistaken! Mama never would have stolen anything from anyone, let alone Grandpa! She loved him! She loved all of her family! She used to tell wonderful stories of when she was a little girl, and how much she loved living here with the rest of you!"

"She chose a peculiar way to show it," Addie said, and that apparently was to be the end of the conversation. She picked up the thick manila envelope from her dresser, where Buddy had seen it the first time she was in this room, and ripped it open with a dagger-like implement.

"Something's very wrong," Buddy said, near tears. "Didn't you ever ask her about it? You couldn't have simply let her go off with a bag holding thousands of dollars and not asked about it when you realized it was missing!"

Addie had pulled the contents out of the envelope and was staring at the manuscript in her hand, her jaw going slack. Buddy didn't think her aunt had even heard what she'd said, and after a few seconds, Addie swallowed hard. "I don't believe this."

"What?" It was Max, still carrying the kitten, rubbing him against his cheek, who had come to the doorway. "What's wrong?"

Addie swallowed again and sank down on the edge of her bed. "Not . . . wrong. Read this." She reached out with the letter to hand it to him, letting the pages of the manuscript scatter across her quilted covering.

Max let the kitten slide to the bed, too, frowning over what he was reading. "We already knew this, didn't we? They want to publish your book, only they want some revisions. What's upsetting about it? I mean, you already knew that, didn't you?"

"No," Addie said, pressing a hand to her chest as if to quiet the tumult she was experiencing. "It's not the same book. This is the one that was returned several days ago. I just took it for granted that they'd rejected it, and I didn't open it, waiting until I figured out where to send it next. And it's a different publisher."

The kitten wandered across the bed, winding up in Addie's lap, where she absently rubbed his ears. Max had forgotten his new pet.

"You mean you've sold two books, in just a couple of days? To two different publishers?"

"I've been trying for years," Addie said, sounding as if she was going to cry. "I have six more books completely written, in that drawer. Two of them I've never even sent out except for the first time. Neither of these publishers has seen any of the others."

Max's eyes widened. "You mean they might be interested in those, too? Holy cow, Aunt Addie. You could wind up a millionaire!"

Addie gave a little coughing laugh. "Well, probably not. But even these two sales will take care of a lot of problems. And if the others are worth something, too . . ."

She looked straight at Buddy, but Buddy knew her aunt wasn't really seeing her. And her own frustrations rose like bile in her throat, because she'd finally asked some pointed questions, and Addie had been too engrossed in her own thoughts even to realize what Buddy had said.

Should she repeat her words? Would it matter if she did? Addie was so convinced that Buddy's mother was a villain—a thief—that she wouldn't even consider the possibility that she'd made a horrible misjudgment.

Max was grinning as he handed the letter back to Addie. "My old man will sure have to eat his words now, won't he? If you get rich and famous, will you still stay here in Hayseed? Or go to the big city somewhere?"

Addie made a snorting sound. "I never lived in a city in my life, or ever wanted to. I don't know a soul in a city, not even Kalispell or Missoula. And the sale of two books, at this kind of price, wouldn't support me very long in New York or San Francisco, or even in Los Angeles, with Gordon. But in Haysville I should be able to do quite a bit with it."

"The way Grandpa's money from the sale of the store should have taken care of him, if it hadn't disappeared," Buddy blurted out. She didn't know where the courage to speak had come from.

This time Addie saw her. "Yes, it would have helped a lot," she agreed. But there was no sign she was admitting that something else must have happened to the money other than its being stolen by her younger sister.

"Did you ask Mama about it?" Buddy persisted, gaining the nerve to pursue it further.

Addie was now looking straight into her face. "You don't give up, do you, Buddy? She'd been home for a visit, and she'd talked about how difficult things were at home, financially. Dan had been off work for several months and only just gone back on the job. She was worried about paying the bills, about affording braces the orthodontist said Bart needed. Thousands of dollars' worth of braces. And Cassie had a fit at the idea of demanding the money back, saying we'd make out all right with Grandpa without it. No, I never asked her. I never had a chance. By the time I'd decided that regardless of what Cassie thought, I would confront EllaBelle, she went and got herself killed in that car crash, and it was too late."

# 15

Buddy was reeling, literally. She backed into Addie's desk chair and sank onto it, not sure her legs would hold her up. "But Mama never brought home any money. They paid for Bart's braces in monthly payments, I remember."

"All I know is that's what she said she needed cash for. Braces. If she didn't use it for that, I don't know what she did with it. But the money was put into that bag, and she took it with her when she left after that last visit. I thought maybe she told Dan she'd borrowed it from us. But he never said anything about owing us any money after she died. Cassie insisted we forget about it. So we did."

*Except you didn't,* Buddy thought numbly. *You still resent Mama because you think she's a thief. And to begin with you didn't even like me because I was EllaBelle's daughter.*

"Addie!" Cassie's voice floated up the stairway. "Mrs. Ballinger's here! She wants to talk to you about that job at the market. Are you still interested?"

"Coming," Addie called, and Buddy and Max stood there looking at each other as their aunt left the room and clattered down the stairs.

Buddy heard the tears in her own voice. "She won't listen. She won't believe me, that Mama couldn't have done what she said. I know it isn't true."

"I guess there's no way to prove anything now," Max said lamely, rescuing his pet as the kitten began batting the pages of Addie's manuscript around. "I'm sorry."

"I'm going to tell Dad when he gets here," Buddy said. "Maybe he'll have an explanation. But I'm sure he doesn't know where the money went. If we'd had it, if we'd spent it, we'd have something to show for it. It was a lot, and my parents didn't buy anything with it. We've still got our old car. We were living in a rented house, and Dad had to keep fixing things that broke down. He never bought anything new that we didn't absolutely have to have."

Max shifted his weight uncomfortably. Then his expression changed, as if he'd shifted gears to his own concerns. "If I tell you something, will you keep it a secret until I'm ready to share it? I don't want my old man to hear about it until I know exactly what's going to happen."

Reluctantly, Buddy let the matter of the missing money and the suspicion of her mother seep out of her consciousness. "I won't give away any secrets."

"The letter from my mom." Max started to grin as if he couldn't help it. "She's met this man she really likes, and they're going to get married. And she says probably I can come and visit them in Texas when school's out."

It took a few seconds for Buddy to work out the importance of that. "Does that mean you might be able to go live with her there?"

"I don't know. She didn't *say* that, but if I like this guy and he likes me, who knows?"

She could see that this was very exciting, and she tried to forget her own anxiety and be glad for him. "That's great, Max. Will your dad let you go? Doesn't he have custody of you?"

"Yeah. But only by default. I mean, he didn't want me, especially. It was just that when Mom left, she didn't have a job or any money to take care of me. Now when she marries Chuck—that's his name—she won't have to work unless she wants to. Chuck wants to meet me. I'll have to tell her about Scamp. I hope it'll be okay if he goes with me. You think Grandpa will forget about him if I take him?"

"He seems to forget about everything else," Buddy conceded sadly. Obviously he had no idea what had happened to his money, or even that it was missing.

Max swept a glance over the scattered papers on the bed. "Imagine, Addie's going to be a published author! Who knows, it may make her so happy, her whole personality will change."

"Maybe," Buddy said. But it wouldn't make Addie realize how mistaken she was about Ella-Belle.

Much later, after they'd had a celebratory supper of Addie's favorite pork chops, baked with sage, onion, and corn bread dressing, Buddy went to bed in her little improvised bedroom. She said her prayers, thanking God for Addie's good luck, and Max's prospect of rejoining his mother, and for the rescue of her father. And in the darkness the thought came to her.

The only way Addie would ever forgive Mama for something she hadn't done was to find out the truth.

Could she do that? She wasn't a detective, and the bag of cash had vanished such a long time ago. Yet if her mother wasn't responsible for its disappearance, where had it gone? Was it possible that it was still retrievable, somewhere, maybe, still in this house?

Her heartbeat quickened, and she added a final

request to her prayer. *God, please help me find it! Please help me clear Mama's name.*

Somehow, with all the other rather miraculous things that had happened today, Buddy felt her spirits rise with the hope that perhaps it was a prayer that might be answered.

Tuesday morning was a letdown. After all the excitement of yesterday, Buddy and Max still had to go to school. As Buddy was leaving, she heard Addie saying to Cassie, "If anyone else calls with a job offer, tell them I'm going to be busy. I have two books to revise, so I won't have time to do anything else. But, listen, Cassie. Even with this money I'll have coming—and it may be weeks or even months before I actually get it—we still have some decisions to make regarding Grandpa. We have to do something different. Getting some extra money isn't going to make him any easier or safer to live with."

Max had gone on ahead with some of his friends. She knew *he* was feeling upbeat. After all, he had the prospect of rejoining his mother early next summer. Knowing that would make the rest of the school year go faster.

And Addie would no doubt revise her manuscripts to the satisfaction of the publishing houses who were offering to pay for them, and go on to sell more stories that would relieve the financial pressures. And she'd keep on believing that Ella-Belle had stolen Grandpa's money.

Aunt Cassie would keep on cooking and cleaning and taking care of everybody, covering up for Gus and Grandpa as best she could, even to the extent of enabling each of them to do things they'd be better off not doing.

And Grandpa—what would become of him? Could they keep him here at home, even if he was likely to start fires or ruin appliances? Or would they have to put him into a rest home where nothing would be familiar, where he would grieve for his own room, his own belongings?

If only Grandpa could remember, Buddy thought, slowing as she approached the school, where everyone else seemed to be walking in pairs or groups, laughing and talking. It was so strange. Sometimes he could remember minute details about the old days, and then at other times he didn't even know whether or not he'd eaten lunch.

School was both confusing and boring. The kids were studying different things than she'd been studying back home, except for math, and while she could keep up there, she felt awkward and reluctant to respond to Mrs. Hope's questions. Worst of all, she had to write an essay to be turned in the following Monday, on the history of Kalispell and early Montana.

Each assignment was different, handed out to individuals written on strips of paper. Buddy stared at hers in dismay. She didn't know anything about the history of Montana. They hadn't studied that in Washington schools.

Across the aisle from her, the girl named Elinor was scowling over her slip, too. "Flathead County in the early days of Montana. Who cares?"

Buddy found her voice. "How are we supposed to find out what to write?"

"Take out books from the library, I guess." Elinor sighed. "Encyclopedias, or history books. Ugh!"

"History can be interesting," Buddy admitted. "If you can find the right books. Well, Aunt Addie's a librarian. Maybe she can help me."

But by the time she got home and asked, Addie said, "I think the whole school's doing Montana history, and every other kid in town beat you to all the best books we've got in our little library. Most of them got the assignment last week. What about the books at school?"

"They beat me to those, too," Buddy said. "So what am I supposed to do now? Maybe I won't have to go to school here very long, so it won't make any difference what kind of mark I get on this stupid essay."

"That's a poor attitude," Addie informed her. "Do the best you can, no matter how short a time you'll be here."

"You might try looking through Grandpa's books," Cassie suggested. "He was a history buff from years ago. The trouble is, a lot of his books are packed in boxes, stacked in his room. He'll probably let you look through them if you want to. I'm sure some of them were on Montana history."

Grandpa, it proved, was quite amenable. He didn't, however, have any recollection of what books he might have on the subject.

"I'll help you look," Max offered unexpectedly. "I have to do some stuff, too. Maybe we'll both find something worthwhile."

So that evening they began to haul cartons of books out onto the dining room table and search through them.

It was dirty, dusty work. Max found several fiction books he was interested in, and set them aside. But there was nothing on Montana history.

Addie, passing through the room, commented, "They're probably all together in one or two boxes. He used to have them pretty well organized, and we took them off the shelves just the way he had them arranged there. Keep looking."

At bedtime, they still hadn't found the Montana books. They had repacked each box they carried out of Grandpa's room and then replaced it in one corner as they took out another. Buddy stared around the cluttered room, where Scamp had followed them and was purring in Grandpa's platform rocker.

"I don't see how he finds anything in here, there's so much junk."

"One man's junk is another man's treasure," Max said cheerfully, opening the top flap on another carton. "Hey, this one looks promising. It's history books, anyway."

He carried the box away while Buddy stood in the middle of the room. Could the opposite be true, also? Could one man's treasure be another man's junk? She wasn't sure that when he'd sold the store Grandpa had been in a sufficiently sound mind even to know that the cash *was* a treasure.

"Did you find what you needed?" Grandpa asked from the doorway behind her.

Buddy's gaze swept over a cigar box, which she'd already discovered held a collection of marbles—from when he was a boy?—and a small carton labeled LOOSE SNAPSHOTS and a small, elegantly enameled container covered with dust. Absently, she reached out and cleaned off the top of it. "No, not yet. We're still looking. This is really pretty. It rattles."

"Belonged to my wife," Grandpa said unexpectedly. "One of the girls gave it to her for her birthday, many years ago. She kept trinkets in it, I think. I suppose I should give it to someone. I'll never use it. You want it, Sister?"

Startled, Buddy swung toward him. "Oh, I couldn't take it, Grandpa!"

"Why not? Old man like me, I won't have any use for it. It's time I was getting rid of some of this stuff, I suppose. Keep the girls from having to sort it all out after I'm gone."

"Gone?" Buddy echoed, uncomfortable with the idea of the old man's mortality.

"How old am I now? Ninety-something? Can't figure on lasting much longer."

She didn't know how to respond to that. She stood twisting the enameled box in her hands, noting the flowers and tiny animals inhabiting a beautiful garden on its cover. "Some people live much longer than ninety-two years," she said finally.

"Not me," Grandpa said, perfectly cheerful about it. "One of these days I'll just go to sleep and not wake up, same way Mama did." He chuckled. "Always got her dander up when I called her Mama. Said she wasn't *my* mama, and I could call her by her name or *sweetheart,* but she wasn't going to answer to *mama* when I said it. Here, open that thing up and see what's in it."

He took it from her unresisting hands and lifted the lid. "Junk," he proclaimed. "Don't know why women have to save all this kind of stuff." He handed it back to her. "Throw all that out and put your own junk in it, girl."

Buddy picked out a pair of earrings that didn't look like junk to her. "They're for pierced ears. Dad would never let me pierce mine. He said not until I was fifteen. And here's a . . . I think it's a hat pin."

"Sister wears hats to church sometimes," Grand-pa said. "You think your little brother would like a collection of butterflies? They're under glass, so they're not dusty."

"Hey, Buddy," Max called, "aren't you going to come help go through these? I think there's things we can use here."

"Coming," Buddy called, then closed the lid on the box to examine its contents later. "Do you really want to sort out your things, Grandpa? And get rid of some of them? Would you like me to help you?" What better way, Buddy thought, to look for the money that might still be resting in all this confusion? If Mama hadn't taken it, as she was sure was the case, where else would it have gone except into a crevice in this mountain of objects?

"Would you?" Grandpa sounded pleased. "Not much in here I really want to keep. Not since I can't see it any longer."

On impulse, Buddy paused on her way out of the room. "Grandpa, do you remember a flow-ered bag, probably about so big," she gestured with her hands, "that you put all the money in when you sold the store?"

For a moment the old man's face twisted in puzzlement, and then it cleared. "Oh. Sort of pur-plish, was it? No, Sister says lavender, not purple. Had pinkish flowers on it."

Buddy was holding her breath. "Yes, I think so. Do you remember having the money in it?"

He looked thoughtful. "Lot of money, wasn't it? Little stacks, with paper bands around each pile."

By this time, Buddy's chest had begun to ache from the tension. *Please, God, make him remember! Don't let him forget again!*

"Yes," she breathed. "I think the bag was full."

But already Grandpa was scowling, as if the effort of recalling was painful. "They kept asking me about it. That silly-looking bag, like something a little girl would carry her doll clothes in. Sister was upset." Suddenly he looked straight at Buddy, as if he could see her clearly, as if his mind had miraculously cleared of the fog that covered it so much of the time. "I wasn't supposed to have given it to her, was I?"

Buddy's words came in little more than a whisper. "Who did you give it to, Grandpa?"

To her dismay, she could see that so quickly the clarity was fading. "Wasn't it you, Sister?"

"I'm Buddy—Amy Kate," she explained desperately. "Grandpa, did you give it to my mother? To EllaBelle?"

"She needed it to carry something. I forget what. She said she'd bring it back. I think she said she'd bring it back. Only I don't remember if she ever did. She probably forgot, and I didn't want it, anyway."

198

Max appeared in the doorway, his mouth opening to speak, and Buddy frantically motioned him to be still. He hesitated, with his jaw sagging, but he didn't interrupt.

"When you gave her the bag, was the money still in it?" Buddy asked urgently. "Or had you taken it out first?"

"Oh, she didn't want the money. Only the little bag. The empty bag. To carry her letters in. She found them in the attic."

Max had caught on to what they were talking about, and though he closed his mouth, he looked almost as stunned as Buddy was feeling.

"Letters," Buddy choked. "Mama put some letters into the bag. And what did you do with the money?"

Grandpa put a hand on the activating button on his talking watch. "The time is 10:22 P.M.," the mechanical voice said. And Grandpa's memory faded off into nothingness. "Could we have cocoa before we go to bed?" he asked.

In the small silence that followed, they heard Cassie somewhere off in the distance. "Haven't those kids stopped poking around in Grandpa's old books and headed for bed yet?"

Nobody reacted to her voice. But Max ran his tongue over his lips and took a step closer to Buddy. "He remembered taking the money out of the bag before he gave it to your mom."

Buddy's voice cracked when she replied. "Yeah. But he doesn't know what they did with it."

Exultation swept over Max's face. "Right. But if it wasn't in the bag when your mother took that away, then it's probably still right here somewhere. In this room. Don't you think?"

# 16

Buddy stared around the room that was packed almost solid with boxes and junk.

"The time," said the tinny mechanical voice, "is 10:25 P.M."

Grandpa was moving toward the doorway, having lost interest in whatever they were saying. Or perhaps he simply couldn't hear them because they were speaking quietly.

Max moved out of the old man's way, his gaze fixed on Buddy while he absently scratched behind the kitten's ears. "It sounds like you were right. Your mom *didn't* steal anything. She just took the bag and left the money behind, only Grandpa forgot about it when Cassie and Addie asked him. He probably doesn't have a clue where it is. But we could look for it."

He followed Buddy's gaze over paper bags filled with clothes and books and heaven knew what else, and all the cartons they'd been looking through for Montana history books. "It might take weeks to go through all this stuff."

"Do you think we should tell Aunt Cassie and Aunt Addie? That it's probably here somewhere, not permanently lost after all?"

Max considered for only a moment. "Maybe not. I'm not sure they'd believe us, anyway. Let's look for it ourselves. That way we won't get them all excited for nothing if we can't find it."

"How are we going to do that without everyone knowing what we're doing?" Buddy asked.

"We could offer to clean up this room, sort things out. Cassie's always saying what a mess it is, fussing because Grandpa won't let her touch anything." Max's mouth twisted wryly. "You'd have to be the one to suggest it. She'd never believe *I* would tackle that much work on my own. She might believe I'd help you."

Scanning the room, Buddy sighed. "It's a big job. But if the money's still here, we have to find it." Excitement began building in her. Maybe she could prove that Mama was innocent of stealing Grandpa's money! "Let's try, okay?"

Not mentioning it turned out to be almost more than Buddy could manage. Max was right, though: Why get everybody's hopes up before they knew the money was still on the premises? Who knew what might have happened to it in more than two years? Grandpa might have thrown it away with the trash without realizing what he was doing.

But Buddy couldn't allow herself to think that way. She *had* to clear her mother's memory. And she would find the money. She hated the fact that she had to concentrate the rest of the week on writing the essay about Montana history, and on other homework, but she didn't dare *not* do it, and Max was busy with his, too.

On Friday evening, over an excellent supper of broiled salmon and herbed scalloped potatoes, Buddy took a deep breath as soon as Gus had left the table—he usually left, without excusing himself, before the others were finished—and spoke the words she'd been rehearsing since Tuesday night.

"Aunt Cassie, is it all right with you if I help Grandpa straighten up his room? He stumbled over a box this afternoon, and I thought maybe if nothing was sticking out to trip him, it might be safer."

Cassie and Addie both stopped eating to stare at her, then at the old man. "That all right with you, Grandpa?" Cassie asked.

"I guess it's time I got rid of some of that stuff," Grandpa said, as if Cassie had never pestered him to do it before. "No sense waiting for it all to be pitched out after the funeral."

"What funeral?" Max blurted, then flushed as Grandpa responded offhandedly.

"Mine, of course. Going to happen one of these days, though old George Hubbard is going on a hundred and one, he told me. 'Course, he's not blind, so he can still read and go for walks by himself without getting lost. I got my hymns picked out, Sister. 'Rock of Ages' and 'Fly Away.'" He sang a bar of the latter. "'When I die, Glory Alleluia, by and by, I'll fly away!' Only need two, don't I?"

For a moment there was a disconcerted silence at the idea of Grandpa planning his own funeral service. Then Addie cleared her throat and agreed. "Sounds about right," she said. "I'll remember to tell Pastor."

Buddy was disconcerted along with everyone else, but she didn't want to get off the subject that was important to her. "It's all right, then? If I reorganize everything? I figured maybe Max would help me lift and move the heavy stuff."

"Uh, yeah, I guess so," Max said, trying to sound reluctant. After all, he didn't want to seem too much out of character.

Right then the phone rang. Buddy didn't care about the interruption, since she apparently had permission to start poking around in Grandpa's room. She held her breath, though, when Max went to answer it, hoping it might be Bart. He was going to call when her dad was finally released from the hospital.

Max returned, looking at Cassie. "It's Mrs. Boardman. She wants to know can you come over and help her? Her father-in-law fell down the back steps, and they think he broke his hip."

"Oh, Lordy," Cassie said, forgetting her dinner. "Tell her I'll be right there."

And so it was that on Saturday morning, Cassie went to Kalispell, driving the car with the new tires on it, to bring Mrs. Boardman home after she'd ridden over to the hospital in the ambulance with her father-in-law. And Addie was preparing to leave for her stint at the library. She looked at Buddy and Max and Grandpa uneasily. "Can you two keep track of him all day by yourselves?" Gus was not yet down for breakfast, but everyone knew *he* wasn't going to be of any help. "Don't leave him alone."

"He can help us," Max said cheerfully. "You can sit in your chair, Grandpa, and tell us which things to throw away and which ones to keep."

"I suppose," Grandpa said, "we could give most of my books to the library, unless Sister wants them."

Addie nodded. "Good idea. Stack all the book boxes in the dining room, and I'll sort them out later."

And then they were left on their own with a

whole, glorious expanse of time to search for the missing money.

Buddy had hoped it would be somewhere near at hand, perhaps having been dumped into a paper bag, whatever had come easily when they wanted to empty the carrying case. But for three hours they pawed through useless, worn-out items of no value whatever. Max went over to the grocery store with the wagon and came back with big boxes so they could pack up the things worth keeping. And he had one box from neighbors in which a new big-screen TV had arrived. They put that on the back porch for the items to be carried to the dump.

At noon they were dirty and tired. They fixed lunch and went back to their task, trying not to become discouraged. Grandpa, after listening to his talking clock, decided he would take a nap, but they didn't stop working. Unless they yelled, it wasn't likely they'd disturb his sleep.

Once in a while one of them turned up something interesting to remark upon, like a collection of miniature ship models thrown helter-skelter together in an oatmeal box. Max decided to ask for them when Grandpa woke up. Mostly, they opened up and hauled out stuff that nobody would have wanted.

Late in the afternoon Max collapsed on yet another box of books and wiped a hand across his face, leaving a dirty smear. "Let's take a break. You want a can of pop?"

"Sure," Buddy said, subdued. "I thought we'd find it before this, if it's here." Her eyes stung. "It *has* to be here, doesn't it? But how can we guess where he'd have put it? His mind wasn't very clear even then, was it?"

"Apparently not. I know they asked him about the money quite a few times after your mom was here and had left, and he never remembered anything about it." Max's voice drifted back from the kitchen. "Is a Coke okay?"

He brought back two cans, popping hers open before he handed it to her. He took a long swig, and then said in a strange voice, "Hey, Buddy."

"What?"

"Maybe we're the ones who aren't thinking too straight. Maybe Grandpa couldn't keep track of things a couple of years ago, but your mom could. Do you think she'd have taken a lot of cash out of that carrying bag and just let him dump it any old place? Where it could get lost?"

Buddy's heart seemed to stop. She set down the pop can because she could hardly hold it. "No, of course not. She wasn't stupid."

"Then what would she have done with it?"

"Something sensible. Whatever it was, I'd have expected her to tell Cassie, or Addie, but apparently she didn't."

"Do we know if they were here when she left?"

Buddy tried to remember what Addie had said. "Somebody saw the flowered bag in Mama's car on her way out of town. Mr. Faulkner, the school principal, I think. Addie thinks he's an idiot, but she says he wouldn't lie."

"But by the time he saw her, she was leaving town, and she'd taken the money out of the flowered bag and put it somewhere else. *Where?*"

"I thought you kids were watching Grandpa!"

Addie's voice was sharp, and they swung around to face the door. Grandpa's bed was rumpled and empty.

Buddy jumped up so quickly, she nearly knocked over her pop can, catching it just in time. "Oh, no! He was sleeping just a minute ago—"

"He's turning up the thermostat right now. Didn't you notice how hot it was getting in here?" It was quite clear that Addie was annoyed with them.

Max muttered a curse and brushed past her in the doorway. "I hope he didn't tear off our stopper again. At least he didn't try to cook anything this time."

Buddy was sorry they'd lost track of the old man for a few minutes, but she had something more important on her mind. "Aunt Addie, were you here when Mama left that last time, right after Grandpa's money disappeared?"

"When she actually threw the bag in her car and drove away? No. It was a Thursday, and I worked at the library all day. She was gone—with the bag and the money—when I got home."

"But the money wasn't in the bag," Buddy said. "Grandpa remembered. They took the money out so Mama could carry some letters in it. Only he doesn't remember what they did with the money."

A peculiar look came over Addie's face. "Letters?" she echoed.

"That's what he said. Letters that she found in the attic. There must have been a lot of them if she needed the bag to carry them."

"Letters," Addie murmured once more. "There was a box of letters she brought down from the attic . . . letters our parents had written to each other, years ago. She wanted to . . . edit them, and put them into a booklet form, so each of us could have copies, maybe even publish them. She said they were wonderful, inspiring letters, and they deserved to be read. . . ."

Addie was looking rather pale, and she sank into Grandpa's chair and put up a hand to massage her throat. "She put the letters in the bag and . . . dear God, could she have put the money into the box she took the letters out of?"

"Where is everybody?" Cassie called out, coming in the back door. "Good grief, Grandpa's been at the thermostat again, haven't you, dear? Max, did you fix it? Addie, what's the matter with you? You look as if you've seen a ghost."

Addie's mouth worked for a moment before she could summon her voice. "Maybe I have. Oh, God forgive me if I have. EllaBelle left the box on my desk, with a note on it to me—something about would I take care of this? I assumed she'd left the letters for me to return to the attic. It seemed like her—careless, inconsiderate, and it made me so *angry!*—oh, Cassie, I never even looked in the box to see if the letters were still there!"

Cassie was scowling. "What on earth are you talking about? I've had a perfectly dreadful, exhausting day, waiting around for June's father-in-law to have his hip pinned, and driving her home practically in hysterics about what she was going to do with him when she had to take him out of the hospital. She's afraid to take time off to take care of him because she'll lose her job, which she needs urgently, but she won't be able to leave him alone, either, and they said they'll have him up and walking by *tomorrow,* imagine! He'll have to have physical therapy, and learn to walk with crutches or a walker or something, but he won't be able to shift for himself for weeks or even months—" Cassie ran out of air and gave her sister a fierce look. "Will you please explain to me what's the matter with you? All of you?"

Addie was consciously trying to calm down, taking deep breaths. "Max," she said. "Your legs are younger than mine, and I don't think mine would work right now. Go up in the attic and find that box that had those letters in it. It's about so big"—she gestured with her hands—"and it had a pink ribbon tied around it to hold it shut. It's probably close to the top of the stairs, because there wasn't room to walk very far into the attic."

Max gave Buddy an excited, half-scared look, then bolted for the stairs.

He was back in only a few minutes, placing the box on Addie's lap, where with trembling fingers she untied the ribbon and lifted the lid.

And there it was. Dozens of small bundles of cash, each with a paper band around it.

Buddy felt as if her bones had melted. When she saw the tears in Addie's eyes, she didn't have the heart to say, "I told you so."

"She put the letters in the bag," Cassie breathed, "and the money in the box, and she expected you to take it to the bank that way. She was in a hurry to leave because they were predicting a storm and she wanted to get home as soon as she could. And then of course her car slid on the ice and—" She swallowed hard.

It was too late to get the box of cash to the bank, and they couldn't think of any better place to put it for safekeeping than to call Mr. Faulkner and ask to put it in the school safe until Monday. For once Addie didn't treat him as if he were the village idiot instead of the school principal, and she expressed her gratitude to him for opening up the school after hours.

Addie had just taken the money off to the school when Grandpa's talking clock announced the hour, and he asked querulously, "Is anybody doing anything about supper?"

After a moment Cassie said, "I never believed much in fast food, it's not very healthy, but today I think we could make an exception. Max, why don't you and Buddy run over to the Hayloft and get us a bag of hamburgers and whatever else they've got to go with them? Gus says they're pretty good. Get enough for the Boardmans, too, and leave them off on your way home. She's at least as worn out as I am. Take enough money out of my purse."

Buddy doubted if anybody really tasted the food except for Grandpa, who demolished two burgers, an order of fries, and one of onion rings.

Addie, when she got back, didn't apologize to Buddy for the things she had thought about her mother. She really didn't have to. Her grief, her pain, were unmistakable. She made no pretense of trying to eat anything, though Cassie insisted she have at least a cup of tea.

Finally, after their fast-food supper, Cassie surveyed the work Max and Buddy had done through the day. "Well, you've gotten rid of a lot of it, but I hope you aren't going to leave it like that. It's still a mess. He'll break his neck tripping over what's left if you don't finish the job."

"Can't we just move those few boxes and do the rest tomorrow?" Max wanted to know. "We're beat, Cassie."

It wasn't until bedtime that Buddy remembered that she'd prayed about finding the money, and about restoring her mother's reputation, and that she'd not yet given thanks for the answers to her prayers. She hoped God would understand that she wasn't ungrateful, just too excited to think straight.

She awoke Sunday morning to the sound of the telephone, and then Cassie calling her. "Buddy, it's your father!"

She practically flew out of bed, not worrying about being in her pajamas. "Daddy? Where are you?"

Her father's voice, sounding normal and cheerful, came over the wires. "Still in the hospital, honey. It's taken longer than they thought it would, but now they say I'll probably get out in a few days, as soon as I've finished this course of IV-antibiotics. Then Bart will drive me to Montana. It was nice of Cassie to agree to have us stay there until I can go back to work, which will be another few weeks, probably. I've talked to the dispatcher at Edmonds Trucking, and they may have an opening at their headquarters in Missoula when I'm ready to drive again. It may work out that the sensible thing for right now is to set ourselves up somewhere near Haysville, so there'll be relatives nearby. The company does some of its dispatching from Kalispell, and that's not too far for me to get home between trips."

"Haysville!" Buddy blurted out, stunned. Did she want to stay here, in Mr. Faulkner's old school, with Mrs. Hope for a teacher, and all those strange kids? Yet, she'd been there two weeks now, and it hadn't been too bad.

"Well, we'll have to work that out. I just wanted to talk to you, be sure you were okay. Let you know I'm doing better."

"I'm okay. Dad, Aunt Addie sold two books for quite a bit of money. And the money that was missing—well, you don't know about it, but the money Grandpa got for the store, that disappeared, we found it last night. Do you remember seeing a little flowered bag—I think it was purple and pink—in Mama's stuff? It probably had some family letters in it."

Dad didn't hesitate. "Yeah, I think I remember it. And the things inside of it were packed away with some of her other belongings, after she died, to look at later. Is it important?"

"Maybe. I'll look for it when we get our stuff out of storage. Mama thought she might try to publish the letters. I'm glad you're maybe going to be here by next weekend," Buddy told him. "You'll be here for Grandpa's birthday party. He's going to be ninety-two."

Dad laughed. "Good for him. I always liked the old boy. Well, I have to go, but we'll see you in a few days, Okay? And . . . I love you, Buddy."

She sucked in a deep breath. "Dad—I hope it won't hurt your feelings, but I've got a favor to ask of you."

"I'm about as susceptible now as I'm ever going to be," he said. "Ask away."

"Could—would you be willing to call me by my real name from now on? Amy Kate? Buddy is such a stupid name for a girl."

There was a silence, and then Dad sighed. "I guess you're getting too grown up to be my Buddy, aren't you? Well, it'll take some getting used to. And I'll probably forget and have to be reminded quite a few times. But I'll try."

She hung up and went to get dressed, feeling happy and encouraged, even if there was a chance they'd be stuck here in Haysville for a while.

She didn't smell anything good from the kitchen. Everybody else was already around the table when she got there, even Gus, though he was grousing because there wasn't any fresh orange juice. "You said you'd get some oranges for today," he complained as Amy Kate slid into her place.

"I didn't have time to think about oranges," Cassie told him. "I was too busy with June Boardman and her father-in-law at the hospital." She glanced at Amy Kate. "June and I went all the way through school together, ever since first grade. I wish there was something I could do to help her now. I'm afraid we're running out of time this morning. I didn't have time to fix anything fancy, so we're just having cold cereal."

"I like cornflakes," Grandpa said. "Used to have them when I was a little boy."

"I like them, too," Amy Kate said, and upended the box over her bowl.

Addie stirred sugar into her coffee. "You know, Cassie, I had trouble going to sleep last night, and I got to thinking. Maybe we could help June and solve some of our own problems, too."

"At least we're not broke anymore," Cassie said, encouraged. "But I don't want to put Grandpa in a home—"

"I *am* home," Grandpa said, proving that he didn't always miss it when they talked about him.

"Of course you are," Addie agreed. "And once the rest of that mess is cleared out of your room, there'd be room for another bed in there."

Grandpa put down his spoon. "What would I want with another bed?" he asked.

"I was thinking that you might be willing to share your room with poor Don Boardman. He's got a broken hip, and when he gets out of the hospital in a few days, he can't come home because his bedroom's on the second floor, and there's no one home to take care of him while June works."

Cassie's mouth dropped open. "But you keep saying it's too much work to look after one old man, so how do we look after two?"

"We hire someone to come in and look after both of them. Two someones, probably. A night-shift person so the rest of us can sleep, and then someone in the daytime to spell you so you can shop and go to church meetings, things like that. Remember how we used to sleep out on the screened porch when we were kids? It wouldn't take much to fully enclose the back porch: windows instead of only screens, and put some sort of heating system out there. Make a place for a live-in worker, maybe. Don may never be able to navigate stairs again, and since his son and daughter-in-law live right next door, they could all visit back and forth as often as they wanted to. It wouldn't cost much to put in a ramp so he wouldn't have to use stairs."

"Easy to put in a ramp," Gus said unexpectedly. When they all looked at him, he added defensively, "I don't mean *me*. Not with my bad back. But I could tell Max how to build it. Or with all that money you came up with, we could hire somebody to do it."

"What a terrific idea." Cassie glanced at her watch, then jumped to her feet. "Hurry up, everybody. We need to leave for church in half an hour. Leave the dishes, just move!"

They scattered in all directions; Max to pour milk into a bowl for Scamp.

"You think they'll make us finish cleaning up the mess this afternoon? On Sunday?" Amy Kate asked.

Max looked at her with a grin. "Maybe, now that everybody's rich, we can talk them into hiring someone to do that, too."

"Maybe not," she said. "Uh, listen, Max—"

"What?" He gave her his full attention now.

"I've decided I want to be called by my real name, Amy Kate. I'm not going to be *Buddy* anymore."

"Good deal. I always thought you were too pretty to be called such a stupid name," Max said, and headed for the stairs, leaving Amy Kate staring after him in total astonishment.

And then, smiling, she went to join the others to go to church.